VASHON HIGH, PLAY|

Written by: Allysha Hamber Cover design by: Allysha L. Hamber

For information contact: Allysha Hamber

Email: allyshahamber@hotmail.com

Website: www.facebook/allyshahamber

allyshahamber@twitter.com

www.myspace.com/allyshahamber

1

Dedication

This book is dedicated to every person who crossed my path (whether good or bad) at Vashon High School. Your presence in my world made High School unforgettable!

To my children: Love is a word that simply is not big enough to describe how much I adore you!

Acknowledgements

Those of you who have been faithful and loyal to our relationships and friendships, you have helped me to unleash a power that my past had buried deep inside me. So to you all, and I know you know who you are because I still keep in touch with you, I thank you so much from the bottom of my heart!

I am moving forward to what God has for me. I feel so overwhelmingly blessed that He chose ME. I don't deserve it by any means and that makes it that more special!

For the gift of persistence, in trying to reach my dream and the hope that despite all my failures, what He has for me is for me and no one can take that away. For His Mercy, that I so don't deserve but He surrounds me with it anyway.

I love you Father for being patient with me, for never giving up on me and for always, always loving me *in spite* of me.

To the two people who ALWAYS are so hyped about every chapter of every book, Linda   and Sherlene Harrison, I thank you both for always believing in me and my talents! I love you both!

To my family: Punkin, Chris, Rhonda, Sherri, Lynne, Taderra, Quionna, Miracle, Chris Jr., Semaj, Uncle Wayne, Chris & Cory, Jessica, Ashley, Robin & LaDonna Foster, Aunt Charlotte and Aunt Bea, Trenton and everyone who's always got my back…I love you all more than words can say!

To those who I have been blessed to meet along the way: Guy Bonner, DaMo2vator, Zabrina, Ruben, Annie, Eljir, Sherree, Myeisha, Shavona, Bryan and the rest of my cast…I got you and I love YOU!

Last but not least, my fans, those who have stood by me through thick and thin….I love you and I'm eternally grateful!

Vashon High

"Playing Hardball"

Prelude…

"…Friends, How many of us have them? Friends, Ones we can depend on? Friends, before we go any further, let's be Friends. It's a word we use every day, most the time we use it in the wrong way. Now you can look the word up, again and again but the dictionary doesn't know the meaning of friends…"

Whodini was taking me and my BFF (Best Friend for Life); through the rush hour traffic on Westbound I-70 headed towards Northwest Plaza. Shopping time! Northwest Plaza was the hottest shopping mall in the STL, other that the Saint Louis Centre downtown. *The Plaza*, as we affectionately called it, held all the stores where you could find the latest hip hop and fly girl fashions. You could find anything you wanted and needed in there, including a new boy toy because there were always out in full force.

As the song bumped out over my Alpine, my girl and I was bouncing, snapping and clapping. Apparently, Whodini didn't have friends like us!

Taneisha (Tae) and I were seniors at Vashon High School, commonly known as, The "V." Vashon was the school anybody who wanted to be somebody, wanted to attend. It sat in the heart of the city, surrounded by high rise projects and low income housing. From the outside, you wouldn't know the old factory looking building was an education facility but inside, it held the best of the best.

Tae and I had been best friends since the third grade at Ashland Elementary School. Our mother's were best friends when we were coming up as well. Tae and I did everything together. We went to church together, after school programs at Matthew Dickey's Boys Club together, we joined the "V's," cheerleading squad together, the student council together and we usually double dated together. We were as close as close could be.

We even went so far as to decide to lose our virginity on prom night together. The key word here is, "together." We stuck together like glue day in and day out. I know they say that blood is thicker than water but our friendship meant the world to me and it was the exception to the rule. She was closer to me than a sister could ever be.

Our main thing in common was that we both had "hoochie," syndrome running through our blood. We loved the fellas and we both had the track records to prove it. We had gone through our share of boys in the hood but being at the big events, gave us the opportunity to expand our "hoochie horizons."

I stood at 5'5, weighing 140lbs, size eleven jeans with perky 36C cups. Caramel colored with shoulder length feathered hair, I had a thing for constantly changing the color of my eyes. One day, they would be blue, another gray and another, they were brown. When I was trying to be fashionable which was always a must, I sported my *Gazelle* glasses. My nails stayed done and French tipped thanks to Lee's Nail Shop in Northland. You know the Chinese would hook you up for $20.

I liked to stay in the latest fashion gear. Guess, Nike, Adidas, Fila, Calvin Klein, etc. Of course it helps when most of your friends are young gay boys who love to boost from the all the major department stores. Hell, we might have been the reason, River Roads Mall eventually closed down cause we hit they asses up almost daily!

I worked part-time at Gus' Men store downtown. I got to see a lot of the local and national celebrities like New Edition, Kurtis Blow, etc.

I kept myself up well. I was in high school with no responsibilities but myself and I loved it. No kids, no little brothers or sisters, just me and my mom.

I dated a lot of guys off and on but once they found out I wasn't giving up no booty, they usually didn't stick around. I was considered "stuck up" but that was cool with me. I looked around and saw how hard some of my other friends had it, being a young mother, having to lug your baby to school with you every day. Missing all the school activities and dances, not to mention how the baby daddy's treated them afterwards and I just didn't want that for myself.

Tae, in contrast was only about 5'2. She was the prettiest chocolate color you'd ever seen. I nicknamed her,

"Snicker's." She was beautiful. Her hair was long almost mid-back length from the Jerri curl she'd worn for the last few years. Her body was well shaped, curves remarkably accented by her choice of gear. She loved to rock anything and everything "Airbrushed" with her latest cliché's. Her personality supported her frame to the fullest.

She knew she had it going on and I admired that confidence in her. You would think a woman like that would aspire for a man who could give her the kind of life style she deserved. Money, fame, glamour but not Tae. She loved her some thugs. St. Louis' most wanted preferably.

Tae said they were rough and exciting to her. Any given day you could ride by a catch her talking to some guy, standing around, throwing up his hood with his fingers. To the hood boys, she was considered prime beef until they also found out that she was stuffing on the goods. Then she too became known as a tease or fake. But it was all good, we didn't mind. We were young and carefree and we held our futures in our own hands... or so we thought.

We were on our way to find the perfect outfit for the perfect shindig…. the "V's" basketball game.

CHAPTER ONE

We had the basketball game on lock in city and the state. We had baller's that would send you home, sucking your thumb and crying like a bitch. Past and Present: from Shotgun and Pistol, them Bonner boys, Gerald Jones, Steve Hall, the Coleman twins, Melvin Robinson, them Nash Boys, Kenneth Simpson, to Sean Tunstall, Vashon represented the best of the best!

People would from all around to watch the game and simply be a part of the electrifying atmosphere which also made it the perfect place for young black sistah's such as us to meet guys. All shapes, sizes and colors. The fellas would show up in their best gear to watch the Wolverines throw down. We had the best mixture for a game that rocked, every time.

We had the Wild Wolves, a special cheering section; the baller's and school spirit that no school in the state could match. From the court to the ceiling, the games were always jammed packed... it was butta baby!

February 1988, a game against our rival, Beaumont High, was no exception. It was at that game, I met a tender by the name of DeAndre Johnson. When I first laid eyes on him, my "hoochie radar," went straight into overdrive. In a crowd of nearly eight to nine hundred people, he stood out.

He was about six four, chocolate covered and fine! I had to get a closer look at him to make sure my contacts weren't playing tricks on me. I turned to Tae and Muffet, our gay friend, pointed to ole boy and said, "Girlfriends, Daddy at three o'clock in the blue and white is lookin' scrumeous! Let's go girls, momma needs a better view."

They both looked at me and said, "Go yo'self!"

I sneered at them.

"I ain't tryin' to look all fast. I'm just trying to see..."

Tae hit me on the leg.

"Damn Lexus, I'm trying to have me an eye-gasm too! You can't be having all the damn fun. Plus I gotta watch my

13

baby get his shit off. You know he can't play right if I ain't watching him."

I waved my hand.

"Girl puh-lease! I ain't tryin' to hear that shit. He yo' nigga for the time being. And he ain't gone be that if you don't give him no ass soon. He gon' be somebody else's boo in a minute," I said, laughing.

Muffet joined in.

"Okkkaaayyyy, Ms. Thang better give him some of them hotcakes fo' he start fucking with waffles!"

Muffet and I slap five laughing.

"Ya'll need to stop. Stephon (A.K.A Money, starting point guard for the varsity squad) ain't going no where! He wants all this *too* bad. Anyway senior prom ain't that far away, he can wait," she said, snapping her neck.

As we all got up to walk down the bleachers and I turned to her and said, "You better hope so! These ducks is quackin' at him more and more every day."

It really was difficult for Tae and me at Vashon. Mostly every girl from freshman to senior was already having sex. Majority of them already had kids. I wasn't trying to be no mother and still in high school. My grandmother raised me and she always told me to respect myself and the boys will respect me even more. She obviously didn't know the boys around my hood!

Peer pressure was deep! I had a couple close calls with temptation but I maintained. I think Tae and I were so popular because the guys were trying to see who could get the ass first.

It seemed as if it took twenty minutes to reach him with all the "hello's and what's ups," we encountered along the way.

Finally as we approached the section he was sitting in, the half-time buzzer was blaring and he was standing. As he turned, he turned directly into us.

Damn! He's finer than I thought.

You see I like a certain kind of man. He has to look a certain kind of way. This guy was thick and he had beautiful bedroom eyes along with thick dark eyebrows and lashes. He was wearing a white Adidas shirt with a crease down the center, (I love that!)

He had on a black pair of Guess jeans, heavily starched with a matching baseball cap, socks and a pair of white Adidas tennis shoes.

This was a look of a man I'd die for. His neck was so thick and his body was so built. His lips were full and looked so kissable. For a split second, I imagined them all over my body. I bet they felt so good. Tae elbowed me to snap me out of my erotic daydream and I slowly extended my hand to speak.

"Hey, my name is Alexis. My friends call me Lex for short."

"How you doing Ms. Alexis, my name is DeAndre but my peeps call me "D." You go to the "V?""

"We all do," we all said at once.

He chuckled.

"Okay, okay I see ya'll reppin'."

His voice was just like his physic, strong and breathtaking. As he turned towards the court, I noticed the two "grand-daddy" diamond stud earrings in his ear. He was laced with gold on his wrists, hands and neck. I immediately thought to myself, *he must be a baller.*

Normally, that would have been my queue to bounce and let Tae take over but he was to fine so, at the moment I didn't care what he did. I was just concentrating on every inch of him.

"You go to Beaumont?"

He chuckled, rubbed his thinly trimmed goatee and looked himself up and down as if to say, *"baby do I look like I'm still in high school?"*

Instead he ran his finger down my arm, sending a tingling sensation down my spine.

"Naw lil mamma, I been out of school for a couple of years now. I'm up at Mizzou. I'm just down here watching one of my folk's take these bums to school."

Heeeyyyy now, a college man! This was definitely a change of pace. He had a head on his shoulders and he was fine? He was definitely my cup of tea.

"And which school does yo' folks' play for?"

He pointed at the court to one of the Beaumont players.

"Number 34, that's my boy."

I in turn, pointed at the score board behind him.

"Umm, well school is definitely in session but I don't think it's us that's getting schooled."

He chuckled.

"A shit talker, I like that."

I smiled and turned to introduce him to my crew.

"This is my best friend slash sister, Taneisha but we call her Tae."

He took Tae by her hand.

"Get it Tae, another lovely name for another lovely lady," he said with a sexy smile.

Tae turned and looked at me.

"Girlfriend, you better snatch him up, quick Boo!"

I snatched her ass up instead and whispered in her ear, "Slow yo' road hoochie, this one's mine!"

I pushed Tae to the side and pulled Muffet closer to me.

"And this is our friend, Muffet."

He kind of gave Muffet this look as if he didn't know if he wanted to touch his hand or not. He looked to me, then hesitantly extended his hand out to Muffet.

"What's up man?" he said, as Muffet gripped his hand.

"Mmmmmm, how *you* doing' handsome?"

DeAndre quickly snatched his hand back and turned to me. He had to clear his throat after one.

"So what you ladi…."

He looked at Muffet before continuing.

"What ya'll doing' later on after the game?"

"Well, usually we all hit up Skate King and hang out after the games. Do you know where that is," Tae asked him.

"If not," I chimed in. "You can follow us."

Tae was always had to get all up in the mix of things, even when it had nothing to do with her. As long as a man was involved, she felt it was her God given right to be noticed by him. She was my girl and all but sometimes the shit got a little irritating.

"Of course I know where it is, I'm born and raised in da Lou, I'm in these streets like potholes baby. I got a few corners to bend with my homies but then we can mob up to the rink, especially if you gon' be in the building," he said, touching my chin with his finger. "If that's aight with you shorty?"

Was it? Hell yeah it was alright with me! Did this nigga know how fine he was?

He was the finest man I had ever laid eyes on and I was a top notch nigga watcher! I had experienced many *eyegasms* over the years so I definitely knew a "hot boy" when I seen one.

I asked Tae for a pen from her purse, grabbed DeAndre's hand and began to write down my telephone number on the palm of his hand.

"Just in case you get lost or can't make it, you can call me later and apologize," I said with an innocent smile.

"Hmm, dig you," he said, looking at my writing. "I got you but uhhh…"

He moved in closer to me. I could feel his breath on my face. My heart began to beat faster.

"It won't be no need for no apologies baby."

I didn't want to move but the crowd was moving and most of our friends mobbed to the hallway to mingle. We turned and started walking away. I knew he was watching me so I swung my ass a little harder and gave him something to see.

Muffet hugged me around the neck.

"Miss Thing, boyfriend was hittin'! You got to see if he has a college friend who ain't ashamed to take the plunge," he said, laughing. "By the way, I won't be joining ya'll ladies tonight. Mother has a prior engagement but I do require full details in the morning love!"

Muffet was a mess. He acquired that name because the fellas said he looked like one of the characters off the *Muffet Show*. He was a little hairy to be a *queen* but he was the one of the greatest friends you could ask for, especially in high school.

Born a boy by gender, Muffet says he always knew he was gay. He said he'd always had an attraction to other boys. It never bothered me that he looked at men the same as I did, it only mattered how he treated me and that was great. He was loyal to our friendship and would back us up, right or wrong. Down to thrown them hands whenever necessary.

His gender parts and maybe the fuzz around his lips were the only indication that he was a male. Other than that, you would swear that he was female to the bone. His nails were longer than ours, his weave was always fierce and he dressed to impress in neutral gear, every time he stepped out the house.

Having him for a friend was a wonderful experience because Tae and I always got the best of both worlds. We could get advice on men and get answers from a male perspective. Everyone at school was crazy about him and respected his choice to be himself and live his life the way he did.

I was lucky to never have had any drama over any man throughout my friendships, not with Muffet nor with Tae but that was all about to change and change quickly.

CHAPTER TWO

I spent the second half of the game staring across the court at Dre,' and Tae teased me for not being into the jumping, buck wild atmosphere. We won the game of course, 92 to 60 and as the *Wild Wolves* chanted, "Beaumont, the door!" Tae and I headed down the bleachers towards the locker room to see Money. Money was Tae's current boyfriend.

I had introduced them to each other because I thought that Tae needed a change of pace. A good man in her life that could be viewed as mellow but still bring the noise if need be. A man that wouldn't just treat her like most nigga's in the hood treated women, like a side of beef.

Money and I were in a few of the same classes at school, sometimes we hung out together after school both with and without Tae. He was different from most of the guys both of us came across because Money was into his studies. Yeah he hung out, he partied, he played around but he was also very serious about his education. Mr. Irons, our basketball coach, was also our principal and played no games when it came to balling on his court and off his court. Besides being nice looking, Money had a head on his shoulders and that wasn't totally rare but not that common in the "V."

Tae was used to dating the drug dealers and the gang bangers; you know the ones who were looking for a baby momma to hold them down because they knew they would eventually end up doing time and would need a bitch to send them some stamps and commissary money, them! They weren't really gelling to well together because Tae couldn't relate to a guy like Money.

To me, he was a prize catch but you know how it is when you try and tell not only your best friend but any woman about her man… they tell you to stay out they business and let them do as they please. Most of them naturally assume you butting in cause you want him, so I decided to hold my peace, to a certain extent of course.

Tae was dead set in her ways and hard headed to the core. She would be one that would have to learn the ways of love like most women, the hard way.

When we saw the team exiting the locker room, I pinched Tae on the back because she was standing next to me flirting with some loser on Beaumont's squad, despite the fact that we were waiting for her boyfriend. A big school spirit *no-no*! She was always flirting with some nigga, especially somebody else's nigga. I always told myself, while I would never allow anybody to just crack her skull, one day some girl was gone make sure she never stepped to her man again.

Anyways, she acted as if she couldn't feel me pinching the hell out of her, so I yelled out, "What up Money? You were housing nigga's as usual! You the man, baby. Give yo' sister some love."

We hugged and he placed a kiss on my cheek as he glanced over at Tae. This dumb bitch was still trying to get her Mack on with the bum from Beaumont. Money turned to me, frustrated and ready to blow.

"Lex, what's up with yo' girl? I know you see her, over there clownin' me in my own damn house? Sis, you better go get her before it get real ugly up in here."

I held up my hand to him. I didn't want to see him get into anything.

"Money, you know how Tae is; you know how trifling she can be sometimes. Just walk over there, snatch her ass up and tell her to bring her ass on."

In my mind I knew I was instigating shit. I could've very well, simply walked over to Tae and told her that her man was about to knock her upside her damn head for what she was doing but I didn't want to. Maybe a part of me wanted to see him finally slap slob out of her. Here most of us girls were complaining about having trouble trying to find a half-way decent man and she treated hers like crap. I mean, I loved Tae to death but she could really be downright disrespectful at times.

I thought Money was simply too nice for that shit. He wasn't the type that would kick off any drama, he wasn't built like that. He would only throw down if he was pushed to defend himself.

Growing up on the West side of St. Louis, Money always knew he'd be a wolverine. His older brothers walked the hallways of Vashon and graced the B-ball court with their presence as well. Yet, with all their talent, none of his brothers made past the high school level in basketball. Namely because they let the spoils of being a basketball player at the most dominating basketball school, take control of their lives.

Ball players were like the twelve disciples'; they were both loved and hated by many. Loved mostly from girls all across the bi-state area and hated on and by, a lot of the guys around town.

It was nothing to find the ball players on the indoor fire escape or the sixth floor, getting serviced by a groupie who would do anything; just because a ball player showed the slightest bit of interest in her. The smell of the fire escape alone would let you know that tons of sex had popped off inside the closed off stairway. Most of the b-baller's had racked up frequent flyer miles on those stairways, as well as the drum room and the closed off sixth floor.

Money was different though. Standing 6'4, caramel, thin framed with sculptured muscles, charcoal colored hair showing the ripples of deep waves and sexy dimples lining his cheeks. Money was one of the hottest thing smoking in Vashon and all the girls let him know at every turn. They would write out their desires in explicit notes, fold them up and slid them through the cracks of his pink locker on the second floor. Tell him about all the things they wanted to do to him if given the chance.

They would slip into the boys' restrooms on various floors and write messages to him and the other b-ballers on the walls. Usually though, only the ones cutting class and shooting dice retrieved them and called.

Money however, wasn't interested in them; he was head over heels for Tae. He often talked about making it to the NBA and taking Tae along with him. Showering her with all the jewels she could ever want. Hell, he already spent a good amount of the money he made working at the *Woolworths* in RiverRoads Mall, on the things she claimed she just had to have. He always tried to buy her everything she wanted.

He cut down on hanging with his homeboys and that was virtually un-heard of in the hood. A crew that grew up together and threw up together, always hung together. They lived by H.O.B (Hood-n-Homeys Over Bitches) all day, every day. Yet Money often brushed them off just to be with Tae. His homeboys' called him a "sucka," for spending all his money on a chick and wasn't getting no sex in return.

Yet, Money loved Tae, I truly believed that. So, I felt that if I had to sometimes push him a little harder to get some type of control over her, then so be it.

We walked over to Tae and Money extended his hand. She looked over at me, looked over to the guy she was mackin' too and then looked back at Money. She had the nerve to have this attitude like we was the ones disturbing her.

"Here I come. Ya'll can wait for me outside, I'll be right there."

"Outside? Girl you better bring yo' ass on, Tae. Don't do this shit tonight cause I ain't in the fuckin' mood," Money told her.

"Excuse me? Who you talking to? Nigga, I said I'll be right there," she said, neck swinging and eyes rolling.

"Yeah homey, she said she'll be right there," the light skinned, skinny guy she was talking too said.

"Hold up playa, was I fuckin' talking to you? You might want to shut the fuck up and get off my court before I slam more than that rock in yo' face."

With in an instant, we were surrounded by all of Money's teammates and their friends. Vashon and Beaumont were rivals far beyond the ball court. Our schools just didn't get along. All it took was for one BlueJacket to pop off at the mouth and the night could end in a full fledge brawl. We had experienced it before, the night ending in tons of police standing in the middle of our court, guns drawn, dogs barking and trying to restore order to all out mayhem.

Money wasn't the type to bang unless you forced him into a corner and the way he felt for Tae along with his reputation, this nigga popping his chops was in trouble.

"Aey nigga, you good?" one of his friends, Cody asked Money.

"Naw, this muthafucka in my house, on my court, trying' to puff his chest out and shit."

Money stared the guy down and bit the inside of his jaw.

"Shhhiiiitttttt, we can handle this nigga for you right now," another one said, patting on the side of his waist as if to imply he had a weapon.

I walked over beside him, reached around him and grabbed his arm. Tae just stood there like she wanted them to fight over her and that pissed me off even more.

"Come on Money, it ain't worth it. Fuck Tae, let her ass walk to the crib."

We turned, began moving through the crowd and began making our way out the gym. As we walked through the parking lot, I wrapped my arm around his.

"Don't trip Boo; you know how that crazy heifer is. I'll talk to her. She just be tripping sometimes, don't sweat it. Tae knows she got a good man, she just needs to be reminded of it sometimes."

"Fuck that Lex, I'm tired of this shit. I spend my time, my grind and its profits on Tae's ass. She don't appreciate shit and she damn sure don't respect me. I ain't never asked Tae's ass for anything. No pussy, nothing! I ain't one of these trifling ass nigga's round here, trying to say whatever and do whatever just to get between her thighs.

But she ain't going to keep making me look like no damn fool. The other week I heard she was up on the sixth floor hugged up with some nigga and if Mr. Ford hadn't come across 'em, she probably would've done God knows what with the nigga. Damn, I love her Lex but she ain't about to keep playing me like no damn fool!"

"Money, yeah she does a lot of crazy shit and yes, sometimes she raunchy as hell but Tae ain't one of these fire escape bitches. We tell each other everything, so I know she wasn't up on no sixth floor with nobody. You can dismiss that one. That stunt she just pulled, I seriously doubt if it ever moves past talking shit. Tae likes attention Money, that's all.

Just go on and kick it with your boys and celebrate. We won and you did the damn thing! Don't let her take that from you. Because of this win, we made the playoffs. Enjoy yourself! You know she'll be calling you later on tonight talking all that shit about how she was just testing you."

I kissed him on the cheek and turned to open my car door.

"Call me."

"Later sis, be careful."

As he walked away, his friends caught up to him and even though he did the ritual of slapping fives, giving out dap, laughing and talking shit, you could still tell that Tae had hurt him and each time she did, it took more and more out of him.

Tae was my girl and all but she was tripping and I was really getting fed up with all her selfish bullshit. I stared off down the strip, reached in the middle console of my car and popped in my LL Cool J cassette tape. He could always make me feel better.

LL Cool J was like the man of my dreams. He was *thugged* out but on a higher mental level than ninety-five percent of the brothers back then. Everything about him turned me on. The words passion, desire and freak hung on his every word. He was the only man I knew that could stimulate women through rap music. He made having sex sound like such a fucking adventure!

As I bobbed my head to the sounds of "I need Love," I saw Tae running out in the middle of the street and towards my car. I pulled over the candy apple red Toyota Camry and threw it in *park*. Before I could open the door and try to get out, she was standing in the front of my car, yelling at the top of her lungs.

"I know damn well you wasn't about to leave me? I know you not acting salty with me over Money's ass?"

I got out, walked around to the front of the ride, grabbed her by the arm of her jacket and pulled her out the street and onto the side walk.

"You need to check yo'self, Tae! What the hell is wrong with you? You can't keep disrespecting that man like that and not expect him to get tired of the shit. Not to mention you'll play him in front of some BlueJacket nigga's? And his boys? Who by the way, already thinks he's a dumb ass for fuckin' with you anyway? You can't keep hurting his feelings like that."

Tae snatched her arm away from me.

"See, that's the shit I'm talking 'bout, Lex. What feelings? Who in the hell want a nigga with sensitive ass feelings? I can't handle that. I need a man who commands me to do right, not ball up like a bitch when he can't."

"Wow... well I tell you what hoochie, keep playing with the man's feelings like that and you just might get yo' wish. You lucky he ain't one of these ignorant niggas' out here that would've just walked up and slapped the crap out yo' ass but then again, maybe that's what you need.

Look, all I'm saying is you know Money cares about you but you act like you to stupid to see that. Contrast to your opinion, he's just the kind of man you need. You gonna fuck around and lose him to one of these skanks out here if yo' ass keeps tripping."

"Why you sweating me Lex? You know damn well Money ain't going nowhere. He'll be calling me later on, whining and shit. Besides, I was just *talking* to the brother. Ya'll act like I was sexing him down on the court."

"Yeah, well who were you on the sixth floor with last week? Yeah, he heard about that too."

"What? Girl, miss me with all that. Lets' just go to the skating party. You know yo' Boo is supposed to meet you there."

"So, you ain't going to call Spider and holla at him?"

"I'll call him later. Right now, let's go get buck."

I shook my head and got back in my car. She was going to have to learn the hard way that her choices have consequences. My choice however, was to head up to Skate King and link up with DeAndre. Tae and Money's drama would have to take the back seat for now.

CHAPTER THREE

Skate King was packed as usual after the Friday night basketball games. It was the closest rink to the city limits for us and basically, just like the White Castle lot on the corner of Natural Bridge and Kingshighway, it was the place to meet up and mingle. Not only with people from your school but all schools. Most of the crowd stayed outside the rink and partied on the parking lot. Somebody always had the music bumping from the trunk of their ride.

I myself came to actually get my roll on, so I went inside. Instantly the atmosphere commanded our attention. We knew the majority of the people there from school or just from being regulars at the rink. The DJ was jamming with "Roll Bounce," playing over the speakers. As we made our way to the rental counter to get some skates we checked out the wall-2-wall honeys; some old and some new.

We were riding high at the "V" when hair styles and fashion were constantly changing. Some of the guys still looked good rocking their Jerri curls from the *Drop Shop*, while others, were beginning to experiment with other cuts like bobs, waves and the famous Gumby (slopped upward to one side). Fashion was doing its own thing as well.

It kept the girls interested but my mind was on a one way street and it wasn't "V-Side" Avenue. I wanted that Dip from Mizzou. I searched and searched for him but I couldn't spot him.

I turned to Tae.

"Tae, you see Big Baby from the game?"

"Naw I ain't seen him but then again, you the one looking for him. I'm trying to run up on a lil something for myself."

"Damn again?" I asked, sucking my teeth. "Ain't you done enough damaged for the night?"

Tae turned towards the counter laughing and responded, "Never Boo."

As I told the young female worker behind the counter my skate size, I felt the touch of a man's hands over my eyes. All I could smell was his *Polo* cologne. I reached up and touched the palms of his hands. They were huge and rough but in a good way. I turned around and there he was. All sexy, dark, handsome, six-foot-four inches of him.

I smiled at him.

"I thought you weren't going to make it."

"And miss out on the chance to chill with one of the finest women in the Lou? No way, Shorty. You skate?" he asked, nodding towards the floor.

"I do a lil' something something," I responded, laughing.

He nodded to the girl behind the counter and asked her for a size eleven pair of skates.

Tae poked me in the side with her hand over her mouth and chuckled.

"Ooooo girl, eleven? You know what they say about them nigga's with them big feet."

I threw my head to the side and looked at her.

"Yeah, I know right. Money wears about a dozen don't he?"

She rolled her eyes. Yes, I was going to rub it in all night.

"So I can't understand for the life of me, why you keep trying to mess that up," I said, pinching her on the arm.

DeAndre grabbed his skates and we all walked over to the bench to suit up. Tae took this as her cue to blow camp and get her groove on. I lost track of her once I looked into his face. He was the most handsome man I'd ever laid eyes on.

The song now spinning on the turn tables was "*Two Occasions*" by the Deele. He stood up on his blades and reached his hand out to help me up. His scent hit my nose like a ton of bricks.

God, he smells so damn good.

This was going to be a hard night for me.

He guided me over to the rink and we hit the floor. Hand in hand, we skated to the sweet sounds of Babyface's voice.

"...a summer love is beautiful but its' not enough, to satisfy emotions that are shared between us. A winter love is cozy but it means so much more but I need so much more. It just intensifies my wants to have a love that endures. Cause every time I close my eyes I think of you...."

DeAndre was getting his fancy on. He was skating backwards, facing me, staring into my eyes and mouthing the words to me. I giggled. He made me nervous and he intimidated every part of me. My legs felt like they were starting to gel. He pulled me closer and told me not to worry.

"I won't let you fall Shorty, I got this...I got you."

His words melted through my body and I felt the hair on the back of my neck stand up. When the song ended, I didn't want to stop but I didn't want to seem desperate either. We skated over to the wall, exited the rink and decided to grab a bite to eat so we could talk a little more and get to know each other a little better.

"So, *Ms.* Alexus, where's your man? I know damn well a shorty as fine as you are has a man, maybe even a few."

I chuckled.

"Damn, a few? Why you say that?"

"You know signs of the times. You women are coming into your own. You ladies took the game from us and re-wrote it, feel me? You look like you could be player material," he joked.

"Actually, I don't have one period, let alone a few. I've been in so called relationships before but they haven't lasted to long. You see Tae and me..." I paused.

I pondered for a moment if I should tell him I was still a virgin. This man was not like any of the high school boys I dated in the past. He was a college man and I knew that he was way to fine not to be swamped with women all around him.

Will he think I'm a baby? Not woman enough for him because I'm not putting out?

I really saw no choice in the matter. I didn't want to begin this relationship no differently than the others, with honesty.

"Tae and I are still fresh meat. "

I waited for his response. He just kind of gave me this look as if he were amazed to hear that virgin's still existed in the world.

"Funny, you don't peg me as a church girl," He joked again.

"I'm not. We just decided long ago not to be like most of the girls in the hood. I for one don't want to be a mother at this age. I got plans and I got goals. I want to become a nurse. I thought that saving myself until I met the right man and graduating from high school, ensures me that the road to that goal would be a little clearer and hurdle free."

45

"I hear you shorty and I must say, I'm impressed. I plan on going to the NFL myself, first round of course. That's my goal. I go harder than every nigga on the team and with good reason, I'm the best," he said smiling.

I returned his smile.

"I bet."

"It's pretty cool though that you ain't trying to have no mini's right now. I wish I would have met you sooner," He chuckled. "I have a little girl, she's two. Her name is DeAndria."

"That's nice," I responded.

I don't know why but the fact that he had a young daughter didn't bother me. Maybe it was because it had no bearing on our immediate relationship. However, I did make myself a mental not to ask him about his "baby momma," a little later on.

As we sat there and talked, I began to feel so close to him. It wasn't really the conversation but more so the attraction I felt towards him. I wanted to touch him, kiss him, hold him and feel him do the same to me. It was something about him that lit a fire deep down within me.

We talked, we skated, we ate and skated some more. By the time it was time to go, hell I was ready to enroll at Mizzou just to be close to him. Tae had gotten a ride home with a one of her other girls so "Dre'," as I affectionately began to call him and I decided to continue the night together. For the life of me, I didn't want it to end.

CHAPTER FOUR

Strolling along side the muddy Mississippi, with DeAndre by my side and holding my hand, was like heaven to me. He could hold a good conversation and that turned me on even more than his physical attributes. We talked for what seemed like hours at a time. We talked about my parents and how growing up without them both had been hard.

"I don't think I felt the effects of my dad not being there as much as my mom. She was only fifteen when she gave birth to me and labor was too hard on her body. Her heart couldn't take the stress and it ended up giving out on her while she was trying to deliver me. My Nana took on the task of raising me."

"The task?" he repeated, chuckling.

"I'll admit, I had some rough spots coming up but mostly because she seemed to always have something negative to say about both my parents.

She used to talk about how fast my momma was and how she probably went to hell when she died for having sex and me before marriage. How she got into the wrong crowd of people after she met my dad. Nana thought he was trash, worthless and should've been in jail because he was nineteen at the time my mom got pregnant. Yes, he was a high school dropout and yes, my mom was only a freshman when he got a hold of her but he loved my mom to death and my mom was crazy about him, too. When he found out she was pregnant, he asked my Nana if he could marry her and she said he'd better," I said laughing.

DeAndre touched my face. He could tell the subject was a little sensitive to me.

"So in order to pay for the wedding and do right by my mom, he began hustling twice as hard, running *Wack* and *Crack* for the some nigga's on the West Side and it landed him in prison for 28 years. He's actually due for parole soon.

Despite the fact that she had always blamed him for my mom's death because he'd gotten her pregnant, Nana use to take me up to Jefferson City to see him sometimes. Then her health started tripping and wouldn't allow her to travel anymore. So, I haven't seen him in quite some time."

"You got a car right? I mean I ain't trying to get in your business and all but what's stopping you from going to see him now that you have your own ride?"

I looked off at the water. I didn't have a ready answer for that one. I guess I got use to him being gone.

"I don't know. I guess I just got use to him not being there and time just kind of moved on. Maybe that plays apart in my decision to wait until I'm married to have sex. For one, I don't want to go through what my mom did and secondly, I don't want be a single parent. I want a man that will share in all the joy with me. You know, like the ones you see on TV when the man's all ecstatic and talking to the woman's belly and shit. I want that."

"I see," he said rubbing his thin goatee around his sexy lips.

"So you looking for a nigga like Cliff Huxtable and shit?"

We both laughed.

"Naw, not Cliff," I said, chuckling. "Maybe I'm just a girl who still believes in Prince Charming."

"Hmm, it's all good Mrs. Huxtable. I might be able to help you with that," he said, leaning in closer to me. "You just may have found him."

"You think so?" I said, loving the way his arms felt around me.

"I know what I'm capable of; it's up to you to find out. Pudding pop anyone?"

He kissed me, so soft and gentle. He stroked my face with soft, loving strokes. Then he began to kiss me harder, more passionately. I wanted him so badly, yet I pulled back. I couldn't allow myself to get all caught up in the moment and make a lifelong mistake.

He looked at me and smiled.

"It's all good Shorty; I don't want anything from you. I just wanted to kiss you. I gotta go back to the campus and I wanted to remember the way your lips felt when I get back."

I smiled. That was so cute to me. He had game, I'll give him that.

"Well, there will be plenty of time for that. Now, we've talked about me all this time, I wanna know about you."

He grabbed my hand and we began walking again towards the grounds of the arch.

"Ain't much too really know. I grew up right here in the Vaughn's Projects. My mom's was a single parent, raising two girls and one boy on Welfare, public housing and food stamps. I guess you can say she did her best with what she had. My pops split before I was born. I just found out who the nigga was when he showed up at my signing party when I signed with Mizzou."

"Wow, that must've been strange."

"Not for me, I didn't have nothing to say to his ass and I had him escorted right out the front door. If I wasn't good enough for him back then, he damn shol' ain't good enough for me now, you feel me? Anyway, I started doing my thang as soon as I was able to multiply and divide. Got into college on a football scholarship and still doing my thing."

I shook my head in agreement.

"My mom is my everything. She keeps me grounded. My baby girl is my rock and my inspiration. Reminds me that I gotta ball like no other so I can take care of her, moms and hopefully you, if you let me."

He turned my face to his.

"And her mother?" I asked.

That's right; I said I was gonna ask!

I wanted to know what kind of relationship he had with her.

"Just some trick I got caught up my senior year at Beaumont. Told me she was on the pill and wasn't. Gold digger to the fullest. She smelled the money and the contracts coming and made sure she was gonna get her piece of the action. Don't get me wrong, I love my daughter with everything in me but I wish I never met her trick ass momma.

I don't even deal with her ass. My mom's get my daughter for me. Outside of that, she's non-existent to me."

I had this frown on my face and when he noticed it, he asked me what was wrong.

"Eww, Beaumont?" I said, trying to lighten back up the mood. Talking about his baby's mother had irritated him to the fullest. I regretted I pushed the issue.

He started laughing.

"Yeah Beaumont Baby. It's all good, I know you V-side."

"Until I die! But I guess I won't hold that against you, Everybody ain't fit to be a wolverine," I said, laughing.

"Grrrrrrr," he growled, pulling me close to him again. He looked me in my eyes and smiled.

"You got beautiful eyes, I like your nose but I'm going insane thinking about kissing these lips again."

He began nibbling on my bottom lip and I swear, I felt the bottom drop out my womb. That's how strong the shockwave was that his tongue sent through my body.

"This isn't making you uncomfortable is it?"

"No," I said, wanting more. "I like kissing you. I'm just wishing we had more time together before you have to go back but I understand."

"Well, why don't you, Tae and Muffuse or whatever his name is, come…"

"It's Muffet," I laughed.

"Well, why don't ya'll all come up to the campus next weekend, kick it with me for a few days. You plan it and let me know. All you got to do is get there."

"Hmm, that's sounds like fun and I know Tae will be down. That girl's middle name is *party*! Besides, I have a feeling she's gonna want to get away for a while after tonight. And Muffet, what can I say? He loves to be on the scene," I said chuckling.

"I'm sure he does. So anyway, umm, I was thinking. I would really like for you come see me in the morning before I leave? Your face is the last thing I wanna see before I bounce. Better yet, why don't you come stay the night with me? I have a room at the Holiday Inn right here downtown."

I shook my head.

"Oh no, I can't do that. I mean,"

"Don't worry, it's got two beds. I'll behave and I'll make sure you do the same," he smiled.

God I wanted to say yes but I couldn't. This was all too soon. Could I trust him? Hell, could I trust myself? I didn't want him to think I was use to doing shit like this.

He kissed me again. This time his soft, wet tongue went down my throat a little deeper. He was driving me crazy. I had gotten so moist between the legs. It was definitely time to go but I couldn't move.

"So you gon' make me miss you tonight?" He asked, handing me a room key. "Let yourself in. I'll be waiting."

I guess he had answered for me and believe it or not, I didn't mind one bit. I could maintain I kept telling myself. So yes, I was going. I wasn't going to pass up the opportunity to lock this sexy nigga down.

"Umm, don't you like; need a ride to the hotel?"

"Oh yeah, my GQ swing got a little deep and a nigga forgot he rode with you."

We both laughed.

"Well, let's make it happen. I don't wanna be away from you too long."

I dropped DeAndre off in front of his hotel and sped home. I couldn't wait to call Tae and tell her about my night. She was going to flip. Besides, I needed her for an alibi.

CHAPTER FIVE

When I arrived home, I walked around to the side of the house and looked through the dining room window of our multicolored brick framed house. My Nana was sitting in her favorite reclining chair, underneath her crocheted blanket, fast asleep. I was late for curfew again and if I woke her, I would be grounded for the next month, at least.

I had left my window unlocked specifically for this purpose. I continued around the back of the house to the other side of the yard. I slowly lifted up my bedroom window and climbed inside.

My foot hit the lamp on my way in and fell to the floor. I paused, hoping the noise didn't startle and wake her up. When I didn't hear anything, I continued on inside and closed the window behind me. I plopped down on the bed and picked up the phone to call Tae.

I didn't get an answer so I decided to page her. While I was waiting for Tae to return my page, I went over to my white dresser, pulled out a t-shirt and a pair of shorts to sleep in. The phone rang and I sprinted over to my nightstand to grab it before it woke up Nana.

"What's up Boo, you just getting home? Oh dish girl, give me all the juice."

It sounded like she was still out partying somewhere.

"Tae, where are you? Why does it sound like you out kicking it or something?"

Girl naw, I'm out just chilling and kicking it with Kevin, you know the hottie from the game tonight? We at one of his homeboy's house, playing dominoes. Girl it's some fine nigga's up in here!"

"Playing what? Girl, you just don't learn, do you?" I asked her, kind of annoyed with her.

I couldn't say anything to her concerning Kevin because I too was about to spend the night with a man I had just met earlier that day also but I could say something to her on the strength that Money was too good to her, for her to be clowning him like she was.

"Please! Don't do me, Lex. You know what I always say; life is a party, so kick off your shoes…"

"Yeah, yeah and live it up," I interrupted. "Did you call my brother?"

"Naw, I'll call him tomorrow. I ain't on that sensitive shit tonight. I'm trying to have me some fun. So don't call the house again cause you my alibi."

I shook my head and let it go. Tae would have to learn the hard way that she was messing over the best thing that could ever happen to her. I would keep my opinion to myself from that point on.

"Ditto," I told her.

"Ditto? What the hell you mean, *ditto*? Where you think you going?

"To the hotel to stay the night with my new Boo. He has to go back on campus tomorrow and asked me if I would stay the night with him. He gave me a key and everything."

"What? So you all in my mix but you about to go stay the night at a hotel with a nigga you just met around the same time as me? What's up Lex? You can't wait any longer? You ready to give up that booty?"

"How you gone try to play me like that Tae? It ain't even that type of party. I kept it real with him tonight and so he knows that the pooh-nanny is on lock and we got separate beds. I don't get down like that, you know me better than that. He just wants to kick it with me before he goes back. Oh, that reminds me... he asked if we wanted to come up on campus next weekend to a party one of his home boys is having. I told him I'm down, what about you?"

"Girl, didn't I just tell you my motto? You know I'm down for whatever."

I heard a man's voice in the receiver telling Tae to hang up the phone.

"Aight Boo, call me in the morning," she said, giggling like a little school girl.

"Aight girl, peace. Hey Tae, call Money."

"Bye," she said, hanging up the phone.

I got up off the bed, finished packing my overnight bag and turned out the light in my room. I walked into the hall way and slowly crept down the wooden floor to the dining room being careful not to make the floor boards squeak to loudly.

I peeked around the corner to find Nana still asleep. I tip toed back around the corner to my bed room and exited the house the same way I entered, the window. I walked around the house to my car, hopped in and was on my way to my man.

I cruised along Martin Luther King Boulevard, to the sounds of Ready for the World's, "Tonight." The words made me second guess what I was about to do.

"… It's getting late, why are you still here girl? Have you made up your mind? You wanna make love tonight? I want you to hold me, I want you to be for real girl please, tonight. Don't want you to go cause I don't feel like being lonely no, not tonight…"

I was beginning to question if I was making a mistake. I didn't want Dre' to get the wrong idea about me and my intentions.

If I go through with this, will he understand that just because I showed up, doesn't mean I want to sleep with him?

I didn't want to make the wrong move but I trusted myself, if I trusted no one else and I knew that I could maintain myself around him, at least I prayed like hell I could.

When I slid my key inside the door, I felt a tingle shoot down my spine. It's something about opening the door and having a fine ass man on the other side, waiting for you.

Dre' was on the bed, stretched out, watching one of my favorite movies, "Sparkle." He stood up, walked over to me and planted a kiss on my lips.

"I thought you were gonna stand me up. I'm glad you didn't."

I smiled.

"Really? I wouldn't do that. Not on purpose anyway. I had to sneak past my Nana to make a get-a-way," I replied as he took my bags from my arms and placed them in the chair. He gestured towards the bed by the window.

"It awaits you Shorty."

He had the bed turned down for me. He grabbed me by the hand and walked me towards the bathroom. I looked inside and he had a bath waiting for me as well.

"First we eat; I got some Chinese take out on the table for a late night dinner. You do like Chinese, right?"

"This is great, Chinese is fine."

He walked over to the little clock radio on the night stand, turned on, "*The Quiet Storm*," and sat down to eat with me. As the radio bumped out the sounds of Surface's "*Shower Me With Your Love*," the words stimulated my soul.

I was getting caught up in the mood of the night and I was afraid of allowing myself to fall into it, head first and then wake up in the morning, regretting it. Yet, I had to admit that Surface was serenading my mind with thoughts of passion.

"…My heart is filled with so much love and I need someone I can call my own. To fall in love--that's what everyone's dreaming of. I hold this feeling oh so strong. Life is too short to live alone, without someone to call my own. I will care for you, you will care for me, our love will live forever. Shower me with your love…"

Dre' looked across the table to me, his expression mimicking what the words seemed to say. That I could have it, if I wanted it. No one would have to know that I'd given up my virtue and loved it, with a man I'd barely known. He grabbed my hand, pulled it to his mouth and kissed it.

"Stop thinking so hard Shorty. Just let the night flow. You safe with me, I promise."

I was so impressed by everything he had done for me. If he was working towards getting my panties to fall off, he was making a great case for himself. I finished my meal, got up from the table, grabbed my bag from the chair and went into the bathroom to bathe.

I sat there in the tub thinking about how nice it was to have a man treat you like a queen. That made me think of Tae and Money. She just didn't know how good she had it having Money as a boyfriend. He was just a great guy.

The knock at the door, gained my attention.

"Cover yourself up for a second Shorty."

I grabbed the curtain and closed it. He opened the door and walked inside.

"I got something for you to slip on when you get out."

"Oh, thanks babe but I bought my pj's."

"I got something for you to slip on when you get out," he repeated, a little more matter-of-factly as he closed the door. "Enjoy."

I snatched open the curtain, thinking he had brought me some little hoochie costume he'd brought along with him as if he knew he'd have some girl in his bathtub that night. I stood up and reached over onto the top of the toilet and grabbed the big terry cloth Mizzou robe, t-shirt and shorts.

Ahhhh, that is so cute. He wants me to dress in his clothes, how sweet.

I exited the bathroom wrapped in his robe and he smiled.

"Every man love to see a beautiful woman walking around in his clothes. I am no exception. Damn, you look good. Come 'mere," he said, patting on the bed beside him.

"Let me tuck you in and we'll re-start the movie."

He wrapped the covers around me, leaned down and kissed me on the lips.

"Umm, you smell good," he told me, kissing me passionately on the lips. "I'd better move before I get in trouble."

He kissed again, hungrier and more passionately. My body screamed for him.

Get in trouble dammit, get in trouble!

He backed away and I looked directly at the big bulge between his thighs. It looked huge. I was so glad he plopped down on the bed before I decided to let my fingers do the walking.

Half way through the movie, Dre' drifted off to sleep. I got up, walked over to his bed and pulled the covers from the bottom of his bed to tuck him in. Before I knew it, he reached up and grabbed me. He pulled me down on top of him.

"Lay here with me Shorty," he said, softly. "I won't over step my bounds, I promise."

I could feel his dick. God, it was hard, so hard and it felt huge against my stomach. Maybe I really wanted him to over step his bounds. He turned me on like I never knew I could be. For a moment, I fought the longing of wanting to know what it would feel like inside of me. I had to get a hold of myself.

This was wrong, I knew it but I couldn't stop it nor control it. I looked him into his eyes. He gazed up at me and told me he just wanted to hold me.

Damn, thanks for saving me, I sighed.

"Okay," I answered, lying down beside him.

He pressed his body close to mine and allowed his jimmy to rest against my ass. He wrapped his strong arms around me, snuggled his chest into my back and his stubby chin against my neck. I loved it and I silently prayed that he would be the one.

CHAPTER SIX

Morning seemed to come all too soon. I'd spent majority of the night, wondering when and if he was going to make a move on me. His hardness stayed pressed up against my butt. He never let go of my waist and he ran his hand up and down my things every now and then. Past that, he behaved and even though that meant he respected my choices and I liked that, I silently wished that he would at least try something!

Rub a titty or something dammit!

I chuckled to myself as I watched him pack. We would have plenty of time for fondling later cause I wasn't planning on letting him go anytime soon.

He walked over to me and asked me the reason I was smiling. I stood up.

"It was just a good night, that's all."

He placed a kiss on my forehead and handed me his robe.

"Why don't you hold onto this for me? That way every time you step out the shower, think of it as if it's my arms, wrapping around you."

I smiled again.

"Aww, that is so sweet. I would love too."

I wrapped my arms around his neck and once again, I could feel his hardness press up against my pelvis. I rubbed my leg across it just to let him know I acknowledged it.

He puckered his lips and I responded with a soft gentle kiss. I slid my leg back across his jimmy again.

He moaned.

"I see you like teasing a nigga, huh?"

I giggled.

"Just letting you know that just because I'm a virgin; don't mean my senses don't work."

"Ump, dig you. Well I better get out of here before I'm late."

He stood back and looked me up and down.

"Woooooaaa," he said, shaking his head and patting his jimmy with his hand. "Down boy! She ain't ready yet," he said, chuckling.

I stuck out my tongue and turned to go to the bathroom. He slapped me on my ass as I passed him.

After we dressed, he checked out and we stopped in the restaurant downstairs and grabbed some breakfast. We walked outside to the parking lot and continued our conversation as we strolled over to his '83 Mint green Cutlass Supreme. I felt a wave of sadness come over me as I watched him throw his bags into the trunk.

He walked over to me, grabbed my bag from me and walked me over to my car.

"I'll call you as soon as I make it back to campus. You got my two-way number, my dorm room number and the payphone number in the hallway. You can always find me Shorty."

I shook my head and smiled.

"You bet yo' ass I can and I will!"

"I really enjoyed kicking it with you and meeting your peoples. Tell Tae I said goodbye and yo' boy/girl too."

"Will do."

He stared into my eyes, came towards me, which backed me up against my car, used his right foot to spread my legs apart and laid his body up against mines. His hands pinning my arms back up against the hood.

He kissed me, hard and passionately, all over my face and neck. He ran his tongue down my chest and between my titties. He nibbled on my nipple through my top. His crouch gyrating across my mommy. I groaned out in pleasure.

It didn't matter at that moment that it was broad day light and we were making out in public on a car. All that mattered was that he wanted me and I wanted him. I raised leg up onto my front bumper so I could feel him closer to my mommy.

He pulled back and smirked.

"Just letting you know that just because I respected the game, don't mean my shit don't either!"

He lifted up from off top of me.

"Aww okay, I see you got jokes too!"

He laughed.

"You gon' miss me Shorty? I'm a miss you."

He kissed me again.

"I do already," I responded.

He opened my car door for me and I slid inside. He closed my door, put two fingers to his lips, kissed them and then placed them against my window. I watched in my rearview mirror as he walked across the lot to his car.

We met up at the exit ahead and I could hear him bumping, The O'Jays, *"Let Me Make Love to You"* in front of me.

I felt my hip vibrate as he pulled out and headed for the interstate. I looked down at my pager and it read, *"don't look so sad, I'll be back."*

I shook my head. This nigga had the game and gone. As I turned and went in the opposite direction, I turned the radio to *Majic 108 FM* smiled as the song connected me to him.

"Just let me make love to you, baby. I won`t stop, I won`t stop til' you ask me to, Tell me to, beg me to. Oh, baby, I`m counting on you, to make this wish come true. If you just let me make love to you, baby. I won`t hurt, I won't hurt, I`ll treat you ever so gentle......"

The words were speaking to my heart and I was thinking that just maybe, just maybe I was ready to go all the way. Everything about him was so romantic and tempting. I just didn't know.

As I turned onto Tucker Blvd., I was caught up in the music when my hip began to shimmy once more. I thought that maybe it was another message from Dre' but it was from Money. He had paged me 911, which meant it was important so I made my way to the Shell's gas station.

My pager vibrated again and again, it was Money. I pulled onto the lot by the pay phone, reach down into the console for a quarter and exited my car. When he answered the phone, by sound of his tone I knew it was about to be some bullshit.

CHAPTER SEVEN

"Hey Money, what's up? You alright?"

"Hell naw I ain't aight Lex. Have you seen or talked to Tae? She ain't called all night and she ain't been returning my pages."

"Briefly, she was hanging out with a few other girls she knew. I went to the rink."

"Wow, I saw her get into the car with you after the game, Lex. Damn, you lying to me now? I thought we was better than that but I guess not. If you was really my peeps you'd keep it 100 with me. What's really goin' on? She was with that nigga from the game, wasn't she?"

I hesitated because I really didn't want to answer that question. I didn't want to be in the middle of their relationship anymore. He kept pressing me for an answer and telling me how it was me who kept telling him to stop allowing Tae to treat him like this so I felt a little obligated to answer him.

"Okay, yes Money but it all was probably innocent. You know, they were just hanging out for a little while and I promise you I left her at the rink, not with him but with a few of her other friends."

"That's it Lex, I'm done fuckin' with yo' girl. I've had it! You and I both know that this ain't the first and damn shol' won't be the last time she pulled this shit. Who in this muthafuckin' town don't know Tae supposed to be *my* girl. She ain't about to keep disrespecting me like this."

I didn't know what to say to him. He was furious and by right, he should've been.

"Money..."

"Naw Lex, I'm cutting the trick loose. Like my man Willie Dee says, I'm a let a hoe be a hoe! That's it. But just cause I'm done with her ass don't let this shit come between us."

"Never that Money, you know that. We was peeps before ya'll even hooked up and we gon' be peeps when it's all said and done. I just wish it didn't have to be like this. I wish ya'll could just work this shit out and get it together."

"Ain't nothing happening, Lex. Let me call her and tell her to pick which part of my ass she feels like kissing!"

I sighed.

Drama was definitely about to come knocking at my front door. Tae was going to be furious but really she had no right to be. I had told her last night, over and over again to pick up a phone and call Money. All this could have been avoided.

She could've called him, smooth things over and then went out and did her thing. It ain't *what* you do; it's *how* you do it. Even I knew that at my age.

"Alright, I know she'll be calling me soon anyway."

He hung up the phone and I returned to my car. Their drama had taken my out of my zone just that quick. Here I was riding high on Dre' and their drama just took me all the way back down.

As expected, about an hour after I got home, the phone rang. Sure enough it was Tae.

"Hello?" I answered.

"Bitch, where the hell do you get off telling Spider that I was with Kevin last night? What's up with that? You played me out for a nigga? I'm your peeps! I been down with you since Pre-K hoe! I thought we were better than that. I can't believe you bitch!"

Click!

She slammed the phone down. I was hurt but I was also a little pissed off. Okay, maybe she had a right to be a little salty with me but she didn't have the right to hang up on me. Especially without hearing my side of the story.

I dialed her back but she didn't answer. I tried again and again, no answer. I guess a part of me did understand why she was acting so retarded. We were girls and we were supposed to always have each other's back. I agreed with this but Money made a really good point when he said I was the one who was always telling him to grow some balls when it came to Tae.

About two o'clock, the phone rang. I hoped across my bed and picked it up. I really needed to explain my position in this to Tae.

"Tae?"

"No baby, it's me, Dre'. What's up Shorty? You expecting a call from yo' girl?"

"Yeah," I sighed.

"What's up? You sound like you got a lot on yo' mind. Everything alright?"

"We kinda just had a few words, that's all."

"I would've thought ya'll was too close for that. Words over what?" he asked.

I really didn't want to inform him too much on the situation between Tae and I because as the old saying goes, "birds of a feather, flock together," and I didn't want him to start thinking that just because Tae clowned like that, that I probably would, too.

"Well, last night at the game, Tae met a guy from Beaumont but her boyfriend Money goes to the "V" with us. So…"

"Don't mean to interrupt you bae, but Tae fucks with ole boy that kept shooting that left hand jumper? Yo, I ain't a fan of the "V' but that boy's gangster with his left. He gone definitely go to the NBA if he stay on his game cause it's rare to find a nigga who can pick which hand he feel like shooting with."

"Right," I began again. "So anyway, after the game he saw Tae talking to this nigga and he got pissed cause he felt Tae was disrespecting him and his court. You know how you athlete's feel about yawl's turf and shit. So, he tried to holler at her, she got flip and we was getting tired of it. The man is good to her but Tae don't like his type. She likes them kind of nigga's that like to control her and talk down to her. I mean, to each her own but I just don't like the fact of her messing over Money like that. I mean, he's a really good friend of mine.

So when he called me this morning and asked me if I'd seen her last night after the game I told him yeah but I also told him that I left her at the rink and I didn't know where she had gone after that."

"Aight, so I'm not seeing the problem. You didn't see her cause we were kicking it, so what's the issue?"
I sighed.

"Well we always use each other for an alibi and I'm sure when he finally talked to her after he spoke with me, he probably let herself dig a hole and say she was with me. When she did, he probably put her on blast and told her he'd already talked to me and knew we weren't together. I mean, do you think I was wrong?"

"I really can't say Shorty. You made a judgment call. Only you know that situation and I'm sure you did what you thought was best. If ya'll as close as I think ya'll are, it'll be aight. She just mad she got caught up. And on the real,

84

she really shouldn't keep putting you in a situation to have to keep lying for her. If she tighten up her game, it wouldn't be no need for it. On a lighter note, you thought about when you coming up to visit?"

I smiled.

"Well, you know I can't stay away too long. So it'll definitely be soon."

"All good. Go on and handle yo' business with yo' girl. I'll check on you later baby."

I hung up the phone and sat back on my bed. I laid my head back against my pillow and thought of what he had said. I agreed with him. Tae shouldn't keep putting me in these situations. I mean yeah, we cover for each other all the time when it came to things like curfew but to keep putting me in the middle of her relationship with Money was just wrong.

I needed to talk to her. I grabbed my keys off the dresser and headed out the door. I had to make her understand that our friendship had boundaries when it came to certain things but Tae had something else in store for me.

CHAPTER EIGHT

I pulled up in front of Tae's house on the corner of Page and Whittier. I walked up to the door of the red brick four-family flat, rang the door bell and waited for Tae to answer. I knew she was home because I could hear her inside talking on the phone. I knocked harder and waited again.

"Tae, come on girl, quit playin'. Come to the door."

Still no response. I walked back to the car, opened the door, got in and sat down. I looked over to the house to see the curtain moving in the front room window. This really pissed me off. Yeah, she had a right to be upset but this was ridiculous. We have always talked about whatever problems we had and this, to me, was no different.

Damn, have I really ruined my friendship with my girl?

I honestly felt I had done the right thing when it came to Money and Tae. I mean, Tae was always tripping. She needed to learn a lesson but at that moment, I just wasn't sure if I was the one to teach it. I just wanted her to grow up and stop disregarding other people's feelings. Especially Money's because he genuinely cared for her.

Yet, it wasn't my goal to hurt her. I loved Tae. I sat there and I began to question, not *what* I did but *why* I did it. I didn't think I wanted them to break up but now, sitting there, I wasn't sure. Maybe there was a part of me that felt as if Tae didn't deserve a guy like Money cause she couldn't learn to appreciate him.

I started my car and glanced over at the window once more. The curtain was still moving. I pulled away from the curb and turned on my radio. I needed to talk to someone who would understand. The sounds of *The Boogie Boys,* took me to the one person I knew would give it to me straight.

"… a fly girl is a girl that's wants you to see, her name, her game and her ability. Two gold chains and cold cash money. The guys are always after her, she tends to act funny. She's got Gazelles and a B-bag too, fly girl, I wanna be with you. You're not the prettiest thing girl but that's okay. Your painted on jeans make you fresh anyway…"

I was bobbing my head to the beat, as I pulled up to the Bluemyer High-rise Projects on Grand Avenue. I parked my car, walked inside the lobby of the building and pushed the elevator button. Muffet lived on the 6th floor and despite the terrible odor I knew awaited me once those doors opened, I was not about to walk up six flights of steps.

When I arrived at Muffet's door, his mother answered and told me that he was in his room listening to music.

"You know how that crazy child is about his music honey."

Even though Muffet and his mother lived in the projects, the inside of their apartment was beautiful. His mother had some of the most unique paintings on the walls and her taste was to me was the bomb. Her furniture displayed earth tones. Bold browns and Crazy Sages.

I walked through the living room down the hall and tapped on the bedroom door to the left. You could hear Prince blasting through the wooden door. I think Muffet thought that Prince had made the song, "Nikki's Grind," just for him.

I entered the room to find an animated Muffet, with a brush in his hand, standing in front of the mirror, going hard with Prince. His shirt rolled up and tucked under the neck line to give him a halter-top look. His mini skirt, flinging from one side to the next and of course his Jerri curl shaped exactly like Prince's.

His room was wall-to-wall Prince. From the *Controversy* album cover to the infamous gigantic, *Purple Rain* poster.

I stuck my head around him so he could see me in the mirror behind him. He jumped.

"Oh, Ms. Fish you scared me half to death!"

I chuckled.

"Yeah I can see you was really feelin' that one."

"Damn right! You know how mother feels about her some Prince! Owwwa!" he said, mimicking him.

Muffet could always make me smile. Now I needed to see if he could help me with all this mess with Tae.

"Muff, I came to talk. It's about Tae."

He came and sat beside me on the bed.

"Do dish!"

"Well, you know how Tae is right, especially when it comes to Money and the way she treats him. Well after we left the skating rink last night, I hooked up with ole boy from the game. I'm a have to tell you about that one later. So anyway, Tae met some character from Beaumont after the game and she and Money had words. Then the trifling heifer went to out half the damn night kicking it with him. Didn't call Money at all, then used me as an alibi and expected me to lie to Money for her but I told him the truth. Muffet I'm tired of her sticking me n the middle of their drama. She needed to…"

"Hold up Ms. Thing," he interrupted. "You saying *she* stuck you in the middle but seems to me that *you* chose to put yo'self in the middle cause you simply could have not answered the phone when Money called. Since when do we cross each other for some beef that ain't even ours? Tae has been yo' girl since Sesame Street and Mr. Rodgers."

"I know but Muffet she can't keep treating him like that. I mean, I hooked them up and I…"

"Right! You hooked *them* up," he interrupted again. "So stay out of it and let them do them. How would you like it if Tae was all up in yo' mix. You wouldn't so you need to stay out of theirs. How you know he don't like being treated like that?"

I looked at him like he was crazy.

"It was rhetorical, fish. Now you got a man to focus on so I suggest you do that cause all this getting in other people's shit is childish behavior and you need to get it together. Don't make me have to read you, seriously. I've always thought of you two as a class act, that's why I hang with you. But you can't have the class if you're missing some of the ass. So I suggest you get yours in gear and fix this situation," he said.

"I'm trying; she won't answer the door or my calls."

"Try harder! Dismissed," he said standing back up in the mirror.

He grabbed his brushed, reach over and turned his music back up and continued his routine.

I headed out the door and began to make my way home.

For two weeks I tried to talk to Tae. I would call her and write her letters in school but no answer. I missed hanging out with her like crazy and I missed our friendship. People kept asking me what happened between us and why we weren't talking. I would see her in the hallways but she acted like she was too busy to stop and chat.

One day after class I saw her talking to Money. I was so relieved that maybe, just maybe this drama was finally starting to be over with. When they were done talking, Tae walked over to me.

"Hey," she said kind of hesitant.

She still didn't really want to look at, me. I tried to lighten the mood a little.

"Hey, I see you and Money are talking. Does that mean ya'll worked things out?"

She looked off to the lockers across the hall, then back towards Money who was standing in the doorway of Mr. Bright's classroom, talking to one of his boys.

"Naw, he ain't feeling me. He ain't trying to hear nothin' I gotta say. He said he's done with me as his girl but we can still be friends."

I winched.

"Ouch, not the still be friends line."

"Yeah, that's what I'm saying," she chuckled.

She finally made eye contact with me.

"You know Lex, you were right. I had a good thing going with Money and I messed it up. I realized over the last few weeks that I really cared about him."

I was glad Tae and I was talking again but I knew Tae all too well. It wasn't that she was realized that she cared about him, she was just tired of seeing all the groupie's up in Money's face and she could no longer do anything about it. He didn't owe her anymore respect and she hated that.

I wasn't going to comment on what she said. I was going to stay out of their drama like Muffet had said but I was going to take the opportunity to apologize and clear the air.

"Tae, I'm really sorry. I wasn't trying to cross you out; not on purpose. I wasn't thinking. I just wanted you to either step up and treat him right or leave him alone. He's my friend too Tae and I didn't want him thinking that I set him up with you and knew you was gone do him in."

"It's cool Lex, you know we always be peeps. I just had to get over thinking that you tried to stab me in the back. So, what's up with you and Big boy?" she asked as we walked down the hall towards the door.

We got to the double doors on the side of the building and got ready to leave. Joe, the security guard asked us where we were headed.

"Wendy's down the street for lunch."

He reached down in his pocket and gave Tae five dollars and told her to bring him back something to eat. He was the coolest out of all our guards and he practically let us get away with anything.

"Oh Tae, he is so cool. We talk on the phone every night and he writes me letters. He still wants us to come up to the campus and visit. He kinda knew we were into it but he said as soon as we worked things out we needed to make it happen. You still down?"

"Let me know when and I'm there!"

We chit-chatted about things that the general public talked about. There was nothing secretive anymore about our conversation. Something was definitely different. Something was missing and I knew what it was…trust.

CHAPTER NINE

My car was in the shop and so Tae gave me a ride home from work that evening. Once again, the conversation was both bland and limited. It didn't move too far past the latest styles at the mall.

About a half hour after Tae dropped me off, I realized I had left my purse in her car on the back floor. I paged her for several times but she didn't call back. About an hour later she showed up at my house with my bag.

"My bad, I was having dinner with Kevin."

She handed me the bag and turned to walk away. That's when I knew for sure that things had definitely changed between us. Normally she wouldn't have been dying to offer me the juice on her and Kevin but this time she had kept her business to herself. Believe it or not, that bothered me.

"I'll holla at you later girl," she said as she jumped back in her car and drove away.

I looked down at my watch to check the time. DeAndre was supposed call at eight. It was now nine forty-five and no call. I called his dorm, his room phone and two-wayed him. Still, I got no answer. I was hoping everything was okay. About ten thirty the phone rang. It was Money.

"Hello?"

"Whad-dup sis? What you up to?"

"Shit, just sitting here wondering why Dre' hasn't called me yet, you?"

"Chilling... I called to see if you wanted to hit the carnival over in Baden with me."

"Umm, I don't know Money; it's been a long day and all this mess with Tae..."

"Girl ain't nobody tripping off Tae. She fucked that up, not you and not me. So I know you ain't gone play me petty over that shit? And as far the long day, you ain't gotta get up in the morning. It's Saturday and you can sleep in. So, let's do this."

"Well," I said. "I guess I can hang out for a minute with my pain-in-the-ass ill' brother.

Money was right. Just because him and Tae broke up didn't mean I had to stop hanging out with him. He was my friend outside of Tae and I didn't want to lose his friendship either.

When Money pulled up to pick me up, I felt kind of weird. I had never felt like that before when we hung out but for some reason this time felt kind of different. I had felt that same feeling earlier while dressing. I mean I couldn't understand why I was paying extra attention to what I had on and how I looked. Hanging out with Money wasn't anything new to me so I couldn't understand why I was tripping. It wasn't like it was a date... or was it?

We cruised down Broadway to the sounds of New Edition.

"...Girl, if ever the goin' got rough, you never were the type to think of backing down. So when you got more than your share, in a minute I knew your heart was in it. I knew that it would make you be your best, put you to the test but if sometimes

it seems like it's not worth the battle. That's when you'll see you can count on me. 'Cause I'm with you all the way. I'll never give up this dream, Although it may seem, There's no way out today..."

It wasn't like we didn't already know that we had a lot in common but tonight felt different for some reason. We talked about everything; Football, classes, movies, music and our goals in life. We had so many of the same thoughts that at times, we finished each other's sentences. It was strange, the atmosphere in the air. It was like we were fighting feeling something, we just didn't want to admit what. After all, he was forbidden, right?

We rode all the rides twice and when he held me or touched my hand the feeling also felt different. We ate a ton of cotton candy and cheese pretzels. Money won me a huge teddy bear shooting hoops. We had a blast. He was like Tae with a penis, meaning I could talk to him about anything and everything and knew it wouldn't go any further.

We were walking towards the Carousel when he stopped me and turned me towards him.

"You know Lex; it was you I was trying to kick it with before you kept pushing me off on Tae's ass. It was you I wanted. It was you I wanted to shower with all this affection and love."

I was in shock at the words coming out of his mouth. Money had never come at me before and I wasn't even sure that he was doing so now. Maybe he was just expressing his thoughts. All I know is I didn't know how to respond, not right off the top of my head.

I decided to just play it off. I hit him on the arm.

"You so damn silly. Why you gotta play so damn much?"

He looked at me and stepped a little closer to me. I wasn't exactly sure why but it didn't make me feel the least bit uncomfortable that he was all up in my air space. After all, it was Money.

"I'm not playing."

He looked dead serious. It was apparent to me at that moment that he was kidding around. I mean I knew Money always thought I was attractive and I always thought he was as well. But we always hit it off as just friends so I never thought of it going anywhere past the point' of friendship. Yet, here he was, standing in front of me and expressing his hidden feelings for me.

"That's so sweet Money it really is but why didn't you say something? I mean you and I have always talked about any and everything. Well, I feel you cause this is kind of different. Truth is," I paused. "I think you aight yo' damn self," I said chuckling.

He grabbed me and pulled me into his arms and placed a kiss on my cheek like he had always done but I'll be damn if Tae didn't come storming up to us out of nowhere with Kevin close in tow.

"Well ain't this about a bitch? No wonder you snitched on me, you wanted him for yo'self this whole time?"

I put my hands up to stop her. She had this all wrong.

"Tae, it's not what you…"

Before I could finish, I felt the sting from the palm of her hand hit me across my cheek. She had slapped me, hard too.

"Oh hell naw, no you didn't!" I said, dropping the bear Money had won me.

I reached back to slap fire back from her ass but Money grabbed my arm.

"Let me go Money!"

His grip wasn't budging.

How the hell you grab me before I get some get back!

"You taking this shit out of content Tae but put yo' damn hands on me again and I swear, it's on! Friend or not!"

"I can't believe you Lex," she said looking to Money and then back to me.

103

"And to think, I thought of this bitch like my sister! Fuck both of ya'll!"

"Tae you getting this shit all twisted!"

"You could've fooled me, Lex."

She turned to walk away. Money stepped in front of me to keep me from going after her.

"Come on Lex, if she can't believe what you trying to tell her, then fuck it. Tae thinks everybody is out to do dirt cause it's what she's usually up too. You can't sweat that. Come on let's enjoy the rest of our *date*. Trip off that shit another time."

We started walking towards the carousel again. I touched my cheek and looked at him.

"That bitch slapped me, Money!"

"Shit I know! I thought I saw skin hit the ground for a minute there," he said laughing.

I looked at him and hit him as we got closer to the ride.

"You know I'm just messing around. You know I ain't gone let you and your girl go Frazier and Ali out here in front of everybody."

As we stood in the line waiting our turn to ride, we continued to joke about the situation.

"For real though," he said. "Who would've won?"

"Shut up, punk!"

CHAPTER TEN

March 20, 1988, the Hearn's Center in Columbia, MO. It was the Missouri Class 4A State Basketball Championship game. We were playing a tough opponent in Lee Summit High School. For the chance to win our fourth state title in the last six years. As I said before, we were a basketball powerhouse.

Muffet and I had decided to ride one of the school chartered buses to the game. The atmosphere on the buses could never be duplicated. We had loads and loads of people heading up to Columbia, including the band, the "Wild Wolves" and the rest of the crew. It was never a dull moment on the road trip.

You could look across the aisle from you and see a couple getting their freak on, cuddling and fondling each other under their jackets. Up the aisle you'd find a crew of girls, gossiping about everybody in town and kicking it together. Someone had always brought along some music so we could get our party on but a bus ride wasn't a bus ride without the infamous "joning session" that took place. I swear you could really hurt yourself laughing at some of the cracks they made on each other's mommas.

This year we carried a 29-1 record into the title game and we knew that with Money, Tunstall, Simpson, Jones, and them Nash boys, we were gonna bring home yet another state title to the "Lou." We were so confident in our game that we had a routine already ready for the final sound of the buzzer.

The atmosphere was live all around me. From my left to my right was a sea of Royal Blue and White. We were reppin' to the fullest. Despite the slamming atmosphere and Muffet doing his best to help me enjoy myself, I felt the void of Tae being there with us.

Money had been great and despite the drama at the carnival and his new found love for being single, he made every effort to make sure our friendship continued on track. Keeping up with his many floozies had become an adventure in itself. It was as if he was running through girls to keep from dealing with what Tae had put him through.

At any given time you could find him sneaking off to the "fire escape," the sixth floor, the drum room or behind the lockers on the fourth floor, getting his serve on. Girls were trying hard to become the next Tae but it was clear, Money wasn't trying to hear none of that.

He was able to run from the bullshit because he was considered "a tender" at school so he had plenty to keep him occupied.

I on the other hand had to fight constantly to keep the dram off my mind. It was always some nosey heifer coming up to my asking me what happened between Tae and I.

I was however excited to watch Money do his thing on the court. It was like watching poetry in motion. He wasn't big on dunks. He was a jump shooter but he love to put his body on you and make you either stop him or get the hell out of his way. Either way, you were definitely going to respect his game.

Muffet and I sat in the middle of the pep club and as I looked down about ten rows to the right, I seen Tae sitting with a group of girls she knew I couldn't stand. She was carrying on and cackling like they were the best of friends. She knew that would piss me off but I refused to let her take me there. The game was beginning and I was determined to enjoy it.

As the starting lineup for Vashon was announced our side of the building went crazy. It was so loud you would have thought we were at an NBA championship game. When the announcer called out Money's name, Muffet and I screamed at the top of our lungs. You could also hear another high pitched voice piercing through the crowd.

"I love you Money! You know you gon' always be my baby!"

It was Tae showing off and trying to save face with the huzzies she was with. Muffet and I stood there shaking our heads.

"Oh nooooo," Muffet chimed. "Tasteless boo… so tasteless!"

We enjoyed a first half filled with dunks from Nash, jumpers from Tunstall and Simpson and lane piercing lay-ups from Money.

Craziness was happening all around us. The cheering section was off the chain.

"...yo' momma don't wear no draws, I saw her when she took 'em off, she threw them on the fence and the birds ain't been back since! Ding dooooonnnnnnggg, ding dong..."

I kept glancing down at Tae, looking like she was having so much fun without me. It bothered me, act or not. A part of me wanted to go down there and snatch her ass up but I refuse to give her the satisfaction. I knew she missed me and I knew she knew she was wrong.

Fourth quarter swirled around and we were ahead 42 to 36. The building was in an uproar as the final minutes began to tick down. We had this one in the bag. We stood to begin our routine we had dubbed for this game.

All eyes fell on us as we began to rock the stands.

"... we are the wolves shuffling through, shuffling on down, doing it for you. We're so bad and we know we're good, blowing your mind like we knew we would. Shooting them jump shots in yo' face, slamming that ball all over the place. Now we didn't come here looking for trouble. We just came to do the state champ shuffle...!"

Yes, we had remixed the Chicago Bears, Super Bowl Shuffle and put our own brand of stank on it. The building went wild. We cheered as the final seconds ran off the clock and the scoreboard read 63-49. We had done it again.

After the game was over and the team took their pictures with the trophy we watched Tunstall cut down the net from the hoop and hang it around his neck. We then waited around outside the tunnel for the team to come out so we could see Money before the buses loaded to head back.

Muffet and I stood on one side of the tunnel while Tae and her little floozies' stood on the other. Through the crowd I could see the team starting to exit the locker room to the shouts and cheer of their fans. I waved to Money and as he tried to make his way to me, the girls were pulling and tugging on him, trying to hug him and kiss him.

He finally reached me and as soon as he reached us, Tae and her clique came up to him and surrounded him. Tae and I had locked eyes for the first time since the carnival.

"Hey Money baby, great game. You was on point tonight!"

"Oh yeah? On point, huh?" he said, looking her up and down.

"Yeah, how about a victory hug, you know for old time sake."

Money held up his hand.

"Different city, same song. I'm good on that. Why don't you go hug that nigga you played me for? Oh yeah, he at the crib watching this on the tube cause he and his squad ain't shit. Matter-of-fact, neither is his girl."

Her so called friends covered their mouths and all you could here was the, "Ohhh's."

He turned to me, wrapped his arms around, lifted me from the floor and squeezed me tight.

"You see yo' boy housing them nigga's?"

Tae's feelings were hurt. I'm not sure if it was from embarrassment or genuine pain. Rather than show it though she snapped her neck and turned to walk away.

"Fuck you too! All ya'll muthafucka's!"

"She'll get over it," he said. "You drove?"

"Naw, we caught the bus."

"Well I did, so I can ditch these hard legs and ya'll can ride back with me. Come on, let's go celebrate and turn Columbia inside out!"

CHAPTER ELEVEN

It was the first day of spring break and Tae and I were still on the rip. It had also been close to a week since I had spoken with Dre'. We had made plans for me to come up to the campus while I was on break and I had already sealed my alibi and gotten permission from my grandmother to leave. Plus, with everything that was going on with Tae and me, I figured it was a great time to get away.

Since I hadn't talked to Dre', if I went on to visit the campus my visit would be unannounced. I decided to go ahead and go. I wanted so badly to take Tae along. This was supposed to be our trip. Two best friends, on a mission to kick with college "hot boys."

I picked up the phone and dialed her number. I didn't know what to say to her when she answered but somehow I would force her to listen and make this right. Her grandmother's voice came over the receiver and she told me that Tae had left for the weekend with her cousin Lisa. Unbeknown to her granny, Tae hated Lisa so I knew that

114

was a cover. She probably had decided to spend spring break with Kevin.

I called Muffet and of course he was all too eager to ride. I didn't know how Dre' would take Muffet coming with me but I didn't want to make the trip along and I'm sure he would understand that.

"Oh yes honey, bats and balls everywhere! Just like mother likes it. Let me make sure I don't forget to pack the oil cause honey these cakes is ready to be greased!"

We both laughed.

"Hit me when you on your way," he said.

I pulled up in front of Muffet's high rise and he came down and got into the car. We chit chatted about making the trip and how it would've been great if Tae was with us.

"She has really been trippin' Muff. I swear when she slapped me, I thought I was gone go postal on her ass. But I understood that she was going through something but she gotta know that I would never push up on Money. We've had this pact since we were old enough to even like boys. Money had been cool with me before they even started fucking around. Hell *I* introduced her to his ass. Told him how she was a good catch for him even though I knew the type of nigga's she normally liked.

I thought he would be good for her, you know, a good change of pace. All she wants is them no good ass nigga's that try to get between her legs and when he finds out he can't, he wanna dog her. I wanted better for her."

"Well child you can lead the horse to the water but you can't make him drink. Tae likes what she likes and you can't do nothing about that. When Tae get tired of seeing the same old program, she'll change the channel. And forget about all that, what was up with Mr. Money expressing himself to you at the carnival? And did you feel the extra love at the game?"

I shook my head.

"Muff, I swear it caught completely by surprise. But I mean, he really didn't say anything out of line. He just told me that he had liked me first and I pushed him off on Tae. And the game, that was just to piss off Tae."

I paused and looked out the window.

"It wasn't what he said, it was the way he looked at me when he said it. I felt something from him that I'd never felt between us before."

"Umm, hard or soft?"

"Huh?"

"Hard or soft? What you felt between ya'll? You that tells it all."

"What? I don't know. Muff you is so damn crazy."

"I know dear," he said turning up the radio. "This my jam!"

He bobbed his head and snapped his fingers as the bass filled the car.

"...*I ain't no joke, I use to let the mic smoke. Now I slam it when I'm done and make sure it's broke. When I'm gone, no one gets on cause I won't let, nobody press up or mess up the scene I set. I like to stand in a crowd and watch the people wonder damn, but think about it then you'll understand I'm just an addict addicted to music, maybe it's a habit, I gotta use it…."*

As we cruised towards the highway, I watched Muffet jamming to the beat and I missed Tae more at that moment than ever before. It seemed wrong to have this much fun without her. I couldn't allow that to ruin my trip though. I would just make sure that when we both returned from vacation that I would do anything in my power to fix our broken friendship.

We turned off Grand Avenue and hit 70 west. We were on our way. I couldn't wait to see the look on my man's face when I arrived at his door. I know I had been upset with him for not calling but I had to understand that college wasn't like high school. He had much more pressure to perform.

What I didn't know was that soon, I was about to find out exactly how much pressure it took to bust a pipe.

CHAPTER TWELVE

When we exited Highway 70 onto Conley Road in Columbia, I started to feel so excited. I couldn't wait to touch him, to hug him and feel those lips again.

It was night time when we arrived and the campus was hitting. There were signs posted everywhere about a party. Come to find the party was jumping off at Dre's dorm.

We found a place to park on the lot. I got out, went to the trunk of the car, reached in my overnight bag and pulled out my makeup bag. I sat back down in the car and pulled down the mirror. I refreshed my face as best I could. I ran my fingers through my hair.

"I hope he doesn't get mad because we just showed up."

Muffet looked to me and then to all the fellas that was passing in front of the car.

"With all this beef walking around here honey, who gives a damn? I mean, really? Who would give a damn?"

"Bring yo' crazy ass on," I told her, stepping out the car. Muffet was right though. It was a lot of hotties walking around that campus. I mean muscles and shit everywhere.

We asked for directions to Dre's dorm and when we reach the lobby and made our way through the gather crowd of party goers, I asked a guy if he knew Dre' and if so, had he seen him.

The guy was buff. He had jock written all over him. He was dark brown and super sexy.

"Damn Muff, we need to hurry up and get to college!" I said, leaning into Muffet's chest.

"Yeah," the man answered. "I hear he's up in his room catching up on his uhhh.... anatomy studies."

He chuckled as he moved to the side and gestured for us to head up the steps. Muffet walked past him and winked his eye. The guy yanked his head back and sneered.

"The fuck?"

Muffet smiled.

We went up to the third floor and walked down the hallway until we reached Room 326. I looked at Muffet and began to have second thoughts.

"You know Muff maybe we should just go back or at least go to a phone and try to call him again. I mean maybe this isn't such a great idea now that I'm here."

"Oh no ma'am! We did not just ride all the way up here for you to get cold feet about seeing yo' man. You here now and you ain't got nothing to be afraid of but yo'self cause you know when he open this door, you gone be trying to give him way more than just a hug, tramp. Now, knock on the damn door."

I stood there and for some reason, I just didn't feel right. Before I could turn away and leave, Muffet knocked on the door, hard.

"Well, I'm a leave you now and go get my mingle on. Holla if you need me, you know for pointers and all," she said, turning to walk away.

My stomach began to get queasy and I thought I was gone throw up. I didn't know why I was so nervous but when the door opened it all made sense.

The door opened slowly and Tae stepped from behind it. Her eye bucked wide open and she stood there in total shock. You could have bought us both for a nickel at that moment.

It seemed like hours passed by with us just standing there staring at each other, out done. She was wearing nothing but Dre's white football practice jersey. Her head looking like she'd just had a wrestling match with about ten different people. My blood began to boil and I pushed past her and made my way inside the room. The bed was in total disarray. The shit had me so dazed, I couldn't speak. I opened my mouth but no words would come out. All I could do was drop everything I was holding, which were my purse and my bag.

Dre' came from out the bathroom.

"Who was that knockin' at the door ba…" he stopped mid-stride when he saw me.

His eyes almost popped out his head. He came walking towards me.

"Lexus baby, what are you doing here?"

His voice sounded one way but the look on his face was saying more like, *what the fuck are you doing here?*

"Never mind what I'm doing here, what the fuck is this bitch doing here?"

I was so pissed off that I was seeing red. I wanted to kill her right there on the spot.

Muffet must have heard the commotion because he walked back to the room.

"Lexus wait, I can explain…."

"Eeeewwww," Muffet screamed and covered his mouth.

When Tae saw Muffet, she dropped her head down inside the palms of her hands. She knew right then and there that everybody in school would know about this one.

"Oh no Ms. Thing, you are all wrong. Not only do you need to be read but you need a severe ass whippin'!"

He looked across at Dre's bare chest.

"And you Mr. Dick-A-Lot! You are so, so very tired! Fine but tired!"

He gave him the famous snap across the face.

I looked over at Tae and I felt livid. I just couldn't fight the urge any longer. I reached back and slapped her dead in the mouth. I hit her so hard I broke the skin on my knuckle. I pushed her backwards and we both fell back into the table. Dre' did nothing to stop it, he along with the crowd of on lookers just sat back and enjoyed the show.

"Get her! Get her Lex! Whoop that ass!" Muffet yelled.

As I tried to pick myself up from up off the floor, I glanced over by the bed and noticed the open condom wrapper. I grabbed it and jumped up off the floor. I was now standing over her.

"You fucked him? You lost your virginity to Dre' tonight? I fuckin' can't believe you, Tae?"

She didn't respond. She was sitting on the floor, crying. Muffet stood shaking her head.

I turned to Dre'.

"And you? How could you?"

"Me? What about you Lexus? I miss a few phone calls cause I got caught up on some punk ass traffic tickets and you fuck that nigga Money!"

"What?"

I was caught off guard with that one.

"That's a damn lie! I never touched Money and Money never touched me! Not so much as even kissed him on the lips. Why would I fuck Money, Dre'?"

I turned back to Tae.

"You lying lil' bitch! That's the excuse you used to get at him?"

I turned back to Dre'.

"That's all it took? Her bullshit ass word and your boxer fell off?"

I walked back over to Tae who was now standing over by the bathroom door. I raised my hand up to hit her again and she flinched. I looked her dead in her eyes.

"Remember what you told me at the carnival? Likewise bitch!"

I turned to walk out the door and passed Dre' on the way out. Underneath all the anger, my feelings were really hurt. I thought I had found what I had been looking for.

"Thanks Ward," I said silently as walked over to my bag. I reached inside and pulled out his robe.

I walked back over to him.

"I don't think that these are the arms I want around me anymore."

Muffet shook his head and we walked through the crowd, out the door and down the hall.

How could she? My best fuckin' friend!

We got to the car and I finally let it out. I began balling right there on the parking lot. Muffet hugged me and tried his best to console me.

"There there now; I know it hurts but I think you handled yourself with class and dignity. Naw, not for real! You went straight ghetto on the bitch and that's exactly what you should've done. They deserve each other honey and you Ms. Lexus, deserves better. So come on fish, let's go find us a motel or something and we can leave out in the morning. As soon as we find his car and key that muthafucka! Come on!"

CHAPTER THIRTEEN

Muffet had to drive because I couldn't stop crying. We had to find us a motel room for the night. I felt so fucking betrayed. I stared out the window as Midnight Star spoke the words of my heart.

"...*sometimes in my life, I feel that I may have, everything I need. But deep down inside of me, my heart is empty. Girl can't you see? Sometimes I'm low in despair, with no one to care. Please, love don't leave me there. I'm so all alone, I have no one to call my own and when I'm weak there's no one there to make me strong. I am searching for love, searching for love....*"

"What a shame honey. *Sparkle* movie rental, $2.99, Gas $30.00, motel $60.00, all those hunks, we'll total them up at about two grand. To see you Ali that bitch the way you did, priceless! Let 'em go honey," he said, rubbing my thigh.

"They deserve each other. Momma knows, get it all out. This is just like last week on "The Young & the Restless," honey. Do you know Ryan and Nina is screwing again? Ms. Thing needs to padlock the monkey just like Tae's trifling ass."

He went on and on until we found us a Motel 6 and settled in for the night. I couldn't wait to call Money and tell what had happened. He was out of town so I had to page him and wait for him to return my call.

When the room phone rung back, I wiped my face and answered.

"Money, its Lex."

He could hear the quiver in my voice.

"Lex, you crying? What's wrong?"

"You will never believe what just happened. I told you I was coming up to the campus to see Dre', right? Well, guess who opened the door when we got here? Tae! *In* his room, *in* his jersey and come to find, she fucked him Money!"

"You shittin' me!"

"No, I wish like hell I was. That hoe fucked Dre'. She told him that I broke ya'll up so I could get with you and that I fucked you. Can you believe that shit? She don't even know him like that. Hell, I don't even know him like that!

There was a silent pause in the conversation and I felt bad. Here I was going on and on about Tae sleeping with someone else. I wasn't thinking of how it would affect Money. He loves Tae way more than what Dre' and I had going on.

"I'm sorry boo, I wasn't thinking. Here I am caught up in my own damn feelings and not thinking about yours. You ok?"

"Hell naw, I'm flabbergasted! I do all the muthafuckin' and this nigga gets the pay off? What kind of shit is that?"

"Money!"

"Money hell; all my hard earned money I spent on that broad and all I got was some titty action? You damn right I'm pissed!"

There was a silent pause again.

"How could she do this to me Money? She had to know deep down that I would find out sooner or later. She couldn't have really thought that we were messing around, that was just her excuse to do what she wanted to do in the first place. We've been around each other for so long. Has it all been a fuckin' lie?"

"I know you hurting baby try not to trip. This ain't shit, it may seem like it now but it's just like water rolling off yo' back. You feel it for a sec but then it falls off. Its better you found out now then later, be thankful for that. I know it hurts and through all my bullshitting around, it's hurting me too but guess what? We better than this and we deserve better than this. So we will get through this, together, you feel me? I promise, I'll be right here every step of the way."

He kept his promise. As spring break came to an end Money, Muffet and I became the three amigos. Money stayed busy with softball, work and school. I kept busy with work and school as well but when time permitted, we all hung out and kept each other company. We went to the

"Request of Pleasure," talent show together as well. As close as we all were becoming, I must admit, it simply wasn't the same without Tae but we made the best of it.

She hadn't return to school after the break and Muffet said that Tae's mom had said that Ta moved to East St. Louis to be with her sister. Letters from Dre' kept coming and I kept forwarding them to the trash. I had no interest in what he had to say. Tae and I however, were different. We had history and now she was gone. I wondered if I would ever see her again.

As prom time approached, I missed her more and more. This was supposed to our time. The moment we had talked about all our lives. We'd been waiting for this day since Pre-K! We'd had it all planned out. Now she was missing everything and I had didn't even feel like going anymore.

Money asked if he could escort me which didn't really surprise me but I thought he'd rather take one of his groupies so he'd be sure to cash in at the end of the night.

I wasn't sure if I should let Money take me to the prom. I mean, people saw us together all the time but they knew we were all really close. To see Money and I at the prom felt a little wrong to me for some reason.

I called Muffet to ask his advice on what to do.

"Honey this is one of the tantalizing days in a fishes life. This is your time to shine. Do you know how many skanks are wishing they were in your shoes right now? Money is one sexy, tall and chocolate; lean yet muscular.... Ummm child' those muscles..."

"Bring it back and focus! Can we be serious for a minute, Muff? I really feel so confused about going to the prom with Tae's man."

"*Ex...ex-man*, honey! And aren't we being a little to June Cleaver to that little tramp that in case you forgot, rode yo' man like The Duke? Girlfriend let me school you about life. It's all about girl power. To be what you want to be and do what makes *you* feel good. Now don't get me wrong, no matter the situation, you would be less than a woman if it didn't make you uncomfortable going to the prom with him.

That's what makes you, you. So now think about *you*. I'm just gone keep it real. You'd have to be blind in both eyes, deaf in both ears and have a body temperature of zero not to know ya'll got feelings for each other. Look at the way ya'll act around each other. Always playing and shit. Hell if I didn't know ya'll I would think ya'll was fucking around already.

We both know good men are not hard but virtually impossible to find. So don't get left behind at the fish market boo."

I sighed. He was right. It was just the prom and why should I have to miss out on my prom because Tae slut-ted herself out?

"Thanks Muff, I knew I could count on you."

"And please let me know if the nine inch rumor is true."

"Muff!"

"Don't act like it wasn't on yo' mind cause you crazy if it wasn't. Now, smooches, the head fish is calling."

I hung up the phone and called Money to accept his offer.

"Lex, I know you. So I know you tripping off me and Tae. But Lex this ain't about me and her; she messed that up. This is about you and me, trying to have a good time on a day meant for romance and excitement. We'll dance, we'll eat, we'll laugh and we won't trip off the rest muthafucka's there, it's all about us. You with me?"

I smiled.

"I'm with you."

CHAPTER FOURTEEN

Money arrived to pick me up in a burgundy limo that he'd gotten from his uncle's funeral home. He was dressed in a white tuxedo that accented his shoulders and skin tone. He had a royal blue cumber bun and bow tie. He was rocking the school colors. I never noticed just how fine Money was until I looked at him, standing in my living room decked out in that tux.

I chose a long royal blue fitting dress with a fish tail. Funny, it was exactly what Tae and I had planned. I'd spent most of the day thinking about her. Where she was, who she was with and what she was doing on what was supposed to be our special day.

Muffet arrived in a fascinating hunter green dress. A padded bra made her breast look real and plump. She sported dyed hunter green pumps with a matching purse. As always, her weaved hair was fierce. She was escorted by a guy from Lincoln University named Wayne.

For a brief moment I thought of Dre' and how it was supposed to be but as Money came over and stretched his hand out to me for a dance, those thoughts quickly went away.

"...as the sun sets and the night goes around. I can feel, my emotions coming down. But now, as hours go by, I cover up my face, saying to myself, tonight I'll forget. Tears, tears... falling down like the rain. Tears, tears, another heart know my pain..."

I was lost in the moment and despite all that had brought us to this point; I was having a great time. I loved Money for doing his best with what he had. I didn't think the evening could get much better.

The announcement of the evening had come. It was time to announce the prom king and queen. As the head of the committee walked upon the stage followed by a few of her students, the gym fell quiet.

"This year's prom king and queen of Vashon High School is, Stephon (Money) Williams and Taneisha Simpson."

I think we both almost hit the floor when their name was announced. It was no surprise for Money to win but Tae, I didn't even think they cast a ballot for her since she stop coming to school. Then again, the girls she was with at the state game were on the homecoming committee so something shady was probably behind her victory.

Money looked at me and smiled. He grabbed my hand and begun walking towards the stage.

"Money I can't go up there. This is not my crown."

"Maybe not but you're coming with me anyway."

We walked up onto the stage and I watched and applauded as they crown Money with his crown. They looked at me kind of strangely, and then looked back to Money.

He grabbed the microphone and began to address the audience.

"V-Sideeee!" he yelled.

"V-Sideeee!" they responded.

"That's what I'm talking about. Shouts out to everybody who voted for me. Umm. As you can see the elected prom queen isn't here to accept her crown but uhh… if you don't mind, I'd like to share my dance with my special queen of the evening. This lovely, lovely lady next to me. Lexus, may I have this dance?"

I smiled the biggest smile. I felt special being acknowledged by Money like that. I walked over to Money, grabbed his hand and allowed him to lead me down the steps towards the dance floor. We passed through the crowd to the barks of his homeboys and the screams of Muffet.

"You go girl, girl power!"

The chosen song for our dance was, *"Make It Last Forever,"* by Keith Sweat.

"…Let me hear you tell me you love me. Let me hear you say you'll never leave me. Ooh, girl, that would make me feel so right. Let me hear you tell me you want me. Let me hear you say you'll never leave me, baby, until the morning light. Let me tell you how much I love you. Let me tell you that I really need you Baby, baby, baby, I will make it all right. No one but you, baby

can make me feel. The way you make me, make me, make me feel…"

I looked into Money's eyes. There was definitely something happening between us. The smell of his Polo cologne, the grip of his hands around my body along with the atmosphere of the night itself made me feel like whatever was happening between us was okay. As we danced, he held me tight and tighter.

"Lex, I know Tae is your best friend, despite everything that's happened I know you miss her, especially tonight but I just want to tell you that there is no one I'd rather be with at this moment than you.

I dig you so much and I've always wanted the chance to just hold you like this. Just once, just tonight, can we pretend that no one else in the world matters except for you and I? Let me be your desire, let me be your fantasy Lex. Let me hold you. Let me just love you totally tonight."

I heard what he said and I was feeling him totally. However, I couldn't. This was all too strange to me. I felt like

I would be betraying her the same way she betrayed me if I even thought about sleeping with Money. The night was magical, don't get me wrong but this was just wrong, wasn't it?

I had already battled within my head and my heart because Muffet was right. I had begun to develop feelings for Money over the past few weeks of hanging out so closely with him. Things kind of just happened as if we were already a couple. We would call each other and see how work went and how homework was going. We would consult each other on rides to and from school, lunch hours and crazy things like that.

None of that bothered me however, this did. It was like crossing a line you could never come back across. My heart on the other hand, I'll admit, longed to know him as intimately as I could, that night and forever. It was a constant tug of war within me.

"Tonight is very special to me to Money. You have been such a wonderful, wonderful escort. You have made me feel so beautiful and like you, I find myself realizing that there is no one I'd rather be with tonight also. I just..."

"I know its Tae, right?" he asked.

"I just feel a little strange. I mean, isn't this all too weird to you too?"

"Yeah, I'll admit, I've been tripping off whatever been happening between us too."

He looked away and I knew that he too, was feeling a little ashamed for feeling this way. I could feel his hands tighten around my waist and if he was holding onto tightly to what could be and I responded and tightened my grip as well.

As Keith Sweat played over the speakers, I think we both were torn over what we felt.

"... *You may be young but you're ready, ready to learn. You're not a little girl, you're a woman. Take my hand and let me tell you baby. I'm yours for the takin' so you can do what you please. Don't take my love for granted, you're all I'll ever need. Hold me, hold me in your arms baby, never let me go...*)

Money pulled back and he looked me in my eyes.

"Um..." he cleared his throat. "Lex, baby I know you loved Tae and at one point I loved her too and God knows I hope you two find your way back to each other. I only want to see you happy and believe or not, I think I've come to the point where I want for Tae too. Yet, despite all of that, I can't help the way I feel about you.

What so wrong about wanting someone? Someone who seems so in tune with you that they finish your sentences sometimes. Someone who brightens your day as soon as you hear their voice. Someone you think about constantly all day and all night? What's wrong with wanting to fulfill that person's every need; wanting to take care of them?

I want to be there to listen to you, talk with you, and offer you advice and just care for you. Lex, I just want to be with you, whatever the cost, whatever the price, I'm willing to pay it."

I stared into his eyes and a tear fell down the side of my face. No one had ever said anything that sweet to me before. Everyone man in my life had just wanted something from me. I thought Dre' was different but he wasn't. My dad was the only man that I knew loved me for just me and now here was a man, who was the pick of the litter, the prize every girl would love to win, who wanted to love me and shower me with his love and I was afraid. Afraid of betraying someone who didn't give a damn about betraying me.

I touched his face. I took my finger and I traced the outer rim of his lips. He leaned in and froze. I couldn't believe this was happening but once his lips touched mine, I felt a surge shoot down my body, straight to my clit. I had never felt anything in my life like that before. His lips were so soft and tender. I opened my mouth to receive tongue. It was warm and sweet.

At that moment I wanted him and I knew he wanted me. When the music stopped, everyone was around us staring and clapping.

"That's what I'm talking about ya'll, do the damn thing!" Muffet screamed.

For the rest of the evening, we mingled amongst our friends; we danced some more and received congratulations' from many people. I'm sure most of the girls didn't mean it but I didn't care. I knew that this was the beginning of the best night of my life.

CHAPTER SIXTEEN

At the conclusion of prom we rode in the limo down to the riverfront to meet up with our friends. We lined the boardwalk and everyone mingled among each other. I leaned up against the limo and watched as Money kicked it with his friends.

"He seems happy," Muffet said.

"Yeah, he does, doesn't he? It's so nice to see him laughing again." I responded.

I sipped on the cup of Cani Wine. I had to sip slowly because Cani would put you on your ass and I wanted to remember every moment of the night. I watched him as him and his boys clowned to music by one of the best new rap groups, NWA.

"*...And all you bitches, you know I'm talkin' to you."We want to fuck you Eazy!" I want to fuck you too! Cause you see, I don't really take no shit; so let me tell you motherfuckers who you're fuckin' with. Cause I'm the type of nigga that's built to last. If you fuck with me, I'll put my foot in your ass. I don't give a* *fuck, cause I keep bailing. Yo, what the fuck are they yellin'? Gangster, Gangster! That's what they're yellin'…"*

They were mouthing the words, grabbing themselves and just having a ball. I bit the bottom of my lip. He was so sexy to me. I couldn't take my eyes off him.

"So? What's it gone be? A lil' far turn back now don't you think honey?" Muffet asked. "I mean, clearly the whole prom saw what I've been telling you all along. He's a good one, Ms. Thing. Don't lose *two* people you love. You hear me?"

I shook my head.

"I hear you."

Money walked over and grabbed me by the wrist.

"Come here."

He walked me over, off to the side and pulled me close.

"You having a good time? I mean is the night all you hoped it would be, giving the situation of course."

I looked at him and smiled.

"It is and it's all thanks to you."

He raised my hands and kissed them.

"I didn't plan on the night turning out like this. I couldn't have imagined in a million years that it would be you on my arm this evening. I don't want anything from you Lex. I didn't rent a hotel room or anything like that. I just wanted to enjoy the prom with you. I can take you…"

"Money, I didn't plan on the night turning out like this either. I guess I've been fighting what's been going on between us but after tonight, I can't fight it anymore. I don't wanna go home. I don't want the night to end."

I kissed him on the cheek.

"Do you?"

"Never," he responded.

I smiled.

"Well, let's go find a room then."

He smiled and tilted his head.

"You sure?"

"I've never been so sure about anything in my life."

The crowd eventually dispersed and Money took me by the house to pick up an overnight bag. We drove out to the Embassy Suites by the airport.

The room was beautiful. It had a king sized bed, a huge bathroom with a shower and a step down tub. There was a see through fireplace in the middle of the room that you could see from either the sitting room or the bedroom. A bottle of champagne sat inside the tub on the table next to two wine glasses. Chocolates were spread about the table and in the bedroom. Roses were on the nightstand. This room was heaven.

I sat my bags down as Money walked up behind me and wrapped his arms around my waist and kissed me on the neck.

"Money, this is so beautiful. This room is too romantic."

I turned to him and kissed him.

"Thank you, boo. I mean it."

"I love it when you call me boo," he chuckled. "Now, why don't you get settled, take a shower and I'll thumb through the TV and see if I can rent us a movie."

I decided to take a bath instead. Those pumps killed my feet and I wanted to soak. I sat down on the tub, staring at the steamy water, I sighed. I had so many thoughts running through my head about not only the earlier evening but what could possibly happen that night.

What if tonight is the night? Am I really ready? And who to say it will be as special for him as it will be for me? This ain't new to him. How am I gone feel afterwards? About him?

Then I heard not only Muffet's but Tae's words ringing in my head.

"Life is a party so live it up! You only get one."

They were right. I wanted some happiness too.

"Knock knock."

I stood up in the tub, grabbed the towel and wrapped it around me.

"Come on in, *boo*," I chuckled.

"You sure?"

"Yeah, I'm decent."

He slowly opened the door.

"Just checking on you; you ok?"

God he was fine. I walked over to him and hugged him. I had one arm holding up my towel and the other wrapped around his neck.

"Thank you Money for everything you've done tonight; for making me feel like a queen. You don't know how good you've made me feel. I seriously thought I couldn't enjoy myself without Tae but you showed me different. I'll never forget that."

"You don't have to thank me. Trust, it's my pleasure."

I started to turn to step into the water in the tub but I turned back towards him. For some reason I felt as if it was now or never. I stepped closer to him. I kissed him. Softly and gently I ran my tongue across his lips as he rubbed his hands up and down my neck and my face. I slid my hand across his back.

In the heat of the moment I let my towel fall to the floor and I grabbed him with both my hands. He looked down at my body. I was feeling no shame, I felt confident he would like what he saw.

"My God Lex, not to sound like a pervert or anything but I have pictured this moment in my head for a long time. You are even more beautiful than I imagined."

He kissed me again and I got extremely moist between the legs. I wanted so badly to feel him. Every inch of him and find out for myself if the rumors were true. I too had wondered for a long time.

"You wanna take a bath with me?"

He smiled a devilish smile.

"That was a trick right?"

I began to remove his shirt. While I had seen his chest many of time before while watching him on the court, never had it looked so firm and sexier than that moment. I had never noticed the handful of thin, fine curly hair in the center before.

I unbuckled his belt, slid it from around his waist and threw it onto the floor on top of his t-shirt. I looked him in his eyes and he swallowed a hard swallow as I unbuttoned and unzipped his pants. Butterflies were swarming my stomach at that point.

I had never actually seen a man naked before but this was one man I was dying to see in his birthday suit. Dre' had turned me on but Money was stimulating every part of me to the point that I think I felt my wetness starting to ooze out from inside me onto my thighs.

Slowly, I began to push his pants down towards his ankles. I admired his abs, his waist line and his thighs as I lowered his pants to the ground. I even admired the silky, Mickey Mouse boxers he was wearing. Mickey's face was resting on place I was dying to visit.

As I passed his jimmy, it caught the rim of his boxers and came downward then bounced itself back to an upward slant and my eyes almost left my head.

Damn his dick is big. Those rumors are so fuckin' true!

I ran my fingers around the front of his boxers and he smiled at the touch of my fingers brushing against his jimmy. As I got his pants down to his calves, my cheek brushed up against the shaft of his jimmy. It was soft against my skin yet solid in its touch. It had left a trace of wetness on my face and I touched my cheek then looked at my fingers.

The clear liquid looked strange yet enticing to me. I licked out my tongue and brushed it up against my finger. The funny liquid had no flavor but it struck my curiosity to go deeper. I had never even held one in my hands before. I had seen girls giving head on TV so I prayed my memory didn't fail me. After all, Money was used to getting head on the regular.

I could hear his breathing getting head just at the touch of my hand wrapping around his shaft. As I touched it, it responded with a jerk. I liked that. I started at the head. I swirled my tongue around it, playing with the juice before running my finger down the middle to his testicles.

I was getting so excited at the way it was responding to me. I brought my lips together and kissed it. With soft, tender pecks before opening my mouth and surrounding it with my jaws. He gripped my shoulders and let out a moan. I like that even more.

"Ummm, Lex wait… this feels….wow, this is some intense shit that's happening right now," he said, reaching down for me. "But, I got to make this right. If you are going to allow me to share this with you, I got to make it perfect. Step into the tub baby."

I stepped over into the tub followed by Money. He grabbed the soap and wash rag. He lathered it up and began to wash me, slow and sensual. Across my shoulders, down my back, around to my chest, squeezing the rag and allowing the soap to run down my nipples. He brushed the cloth against them and nipples came out to play, so hard and erect. He continued down my waist and around my hips.

Tenderly he bathed my mommy like a mother bathing her newborn child. No aggression, just pure gentleness as he moved the rag back and forth across my lips. The more he washed, the more stimulated I became. As he cleaned my opening, he kissed me across my face and down my neck. I could feel his harness against my stomach and I almost jumped him right there in the tub. My mommy was pounding with want on the inside.

He slid down to the water and wet the towel and began to rinse me. I took the rag from him to return the favor. I began to wash his chest. I washed his arms and his back. I ran the rag up and down his thighs; taking it and wrapping it around his jimmy. I began to make circles around it and I could feel it swell and pulsate in my hand.

He moaned out in approval. Round and round I went, dying to feel it inside me.

I rinsed him off and he stepped out the tub.

"Wait here until I call you, K?"

"Why? Money I'm ready," I said looking confused.

"Please just wait."

He left the bathroom and I got out of the tub, grabbed a towel, wrapped it around myself and walked over to the vanity mirror. I wanted to make sure I still looked okay for the big moment.

I grabbed my comb, toyed with my hair then grabbed my make up bag to retrieve my lip liner. As I re-lined my lips, I thought back to Tae. I never used to line my lips until she told me the boys liked it.

"You have got to be kidding," I said to her as she put on the brown lip liner she'd just bought. "It looks kind of funny to me."

"No it don't girl, it makes your lips look fuller. Trust me the boys love full lips."

I really missed her.

"Come with me," I heard him say.

Money had come back into the bathroom and with the sound of his voice; Tae's face along with everything else disappeared from my mind.

CHAPTER SEVENTEEN

When I walked into the room, Money un-covered my eyes. He had lit an incense, turned on the *Quiet Storm*, poured some champagne and dimmed the lights. He had taken apart a few of my roses and made a trail to the bed. He handed me a glass of champagne and lifted his.

"To tonight... to dreams coming true."

He wrapped his arm around mine and we sipped the wine as we stared into each other's eyes.

"Dance with me," he said.

He took me to the middle of the floor and placed his hand on the small of my back. The Quiet Storm was playing "Choosey Lover," by the Isley Brothers.

"...Thought I had a lover but I was kiddin' myself, baby. By the time I learned the truth about it, she was sleepin' with someone else, oh, but not you, baby. Choosey lover, Girl, I'm so proud of you. I'm so glad you chose me, baby and I'll make you so happy..."

"Ain't that some shit? Perfect song," he said, chuckling.

As we danced, we kissed, we touched and we totally fell deeper into each other. He went to dip me and my towel fell to the floor. He looked down to my breast and he leaned in and planted the wettest kiss on my nipple. He brought his hand up to grip them. He squeezed with aggression but kissed them tenderly; a hell-of-a combination.

He raised me and looked down into my eyes. He backed me up over to the wall and threw my hands above my head. It was my breathing now that was getting heavier by the second. He kissed me on the neck, much hungrier this time and went down to my breast.

He nibbled from one to the other. Sucking them like a newborn starving for milk. I thought my knees would buckle it felt so damn good. He released my hands but instructed me not to touch him. He slid his tongue down my waist and placed it into my navel.

He slid his hand down around my thighs and rubbed his thumb across my clit. I gasped at the feel of his touch between my legs. I swallowed hard as he gripped my thigh with his hand and lifted my leg up onto a nearby chair. He was on his knees and he began to massage my clit with both his thumbs. It sounds crazy but I wanted to cry from the intensity I felt between my legs.

He leaned in and placed his soft, wet tongue on my clit. It was one the strangest feelings I'd ever felt. It felt like his tongue was tickling me and wouldn't stop. I didn't want to laugh though; I wanted to scream out in pleasure.

I bowled over and grabbed his shoulders.

"No touching," he reminded me.

I gripped my hands together and squeezed. I didn't know what else to do. The feeling I felt kept mounting and building. I could feel something crazy and exciting happening to me and I didn't know how to handle it. My breathing was out of control and I felt this pressure telling me to push down and scream. I gripped his head. He moaned because he knew what was coming, I didn't.

I screamed out his name.

"Money, Money, what is that? What are you doing? Oh, it feels good, awww, I feel like I about to explode. My body is so...so hot...what ...is ... tthhiiiiiiisssssssss?"

I began hitting Money on his back. I let it go and the feeling felt so good it scared me. I pushed Money away from and I ran into the bathroom to make sure I didn't pee on myself. My heart was racing; my body was doing all kinds of shit I never knew was possible. I was tingling from head to toe and I wanted more of it. It was crazy. My legs were weak and shaking. I sat down on the toilet and waited for things to calm down.

Money came and stood in the doorway, smiling and biting down on his bottom lip.

"You good?"

I could barely get it out.

"I think so," I said, still breathing hard. "What the hell?"

He walked over to me and kneeled down in front of me.

I looked at him, my eyes spaced out and my heart fluttering.

"It's okay baby. You just experienced your first orgasm, that's all."

He leaned in and kissed me. He raised his body and kissed me passionately. I could taste my juices on his lips and tongue and the flavor seemed to excite me. I grabbed him around his neck and he slid me off the toilet onto his lap.

I pulled back.

"So, that's what it feels like?"

He looked at me and smiled.

"Why don't we do it again just to make sure?"

He picked me up and took me back into the room and over to the bed. My body felt as if it was still having spasms. He laid me down on the bed and towered above me. He looked so intimidating above me but he was a gentle as an angel.

He leaned in to kiss me, his hands traveling all over my body. He took his finger and rubbed it across the opening of my mommy. It was so wet I could hear it popping. He was gentle with me as he slid his finger inside. His tongue swimming in my mouth. The combination was intense and I loved it.

"...We started out simple friends. That kind of friendship never ends, no baby. But we were fortunate to care enough, we knew just where we stood but soon as love appeared, you turned away. And you were so unsure and so afraid of feeling what I was feeling. You were scared that love would blow your heart away..."

He worked his finger inside, a little deeper.

"... And you were certain that in time my love would stray..."

My nails went into his skin. My body responding with gyration.

"... *Where, where will you go and who, who's gonna love you like I do...*"

"You ready"

"Yes," I moaned. "But not for that. I'm ready to please you."

I rolled him on his back and began kissing him on his neck. I nibbled on his chin and on up to his bottom lip. He brought his hand up and placed the finger he had just removed from inside me, into his mouth. I stuck my tongue into his mouth to share the flavor.

I moved down to his chest. Placing kisses down his mid-section. I reached his jimmy and I picked it up, wet my lips and began to kiss it as if I was kissing his lips. I started at the top, made my way down the side and then back up to the top. I wasn't the best but his reactions made me feel as if I was the bomb. He was moaning, squeezing my arms and saying some of the sexiest and nastiest things to me.

"Baby," he whispered. "Are you sure you wanna do this? I don't want you to feel pressure in any way to go through with this. I..."

I rose up to him.

"Shhh... Money, I want you right now more than anything in the world. This is the only level of satisfaction I haven't felt tonight and I wanna feel it."

He got off the bed. I watched as he went over to the dresser, got his wallet and retrieved a condom. I swallowed a hard swallow and the butterflies began to return. Yet when he lay down beside me, they were obsolete.

He looked me into my eyes and I could see that this man really did care about me. That everything he said to me came straight from his heart. I pulled him closer to me. He rolled on top of me and used his knee to push my legs apart.

The moment had come. He leaned down in my ear and began to talk me through it.

"I want you."

166

I felt the head of his jimmy greet the opening of my mommy.

"I've wanted you from jump."

I gasped as the tip of his jimmy began to push inside me. I gasped because I could begin to feel the pressure and a little pain.

"Put you arms around me; hold me baby."

I felt it piercing my walls. The head felt humongous.

"Squeeze me; bite me if you have too. Close your eyes baby. Enjoy Heaven with me."

My moans began very vocal and my breathing labored. It was close and it hurt like hell. I did as he instructed and I dug into him with my hands and nails.

"Oh my God, oh my God."

"You okay baby," he said looking at me.

I looked at him and I felt a tear roll down the side of my face. He caught it with his lips.

"You don't have to do this Lex."

"Don't stop."

He moved into me closer and closer and closer. I felt the pressure and the pain began to ease and slowly he talked me into pleasure. His voice was not only soothing but inviting. He made me want to fuck him despite the pain and as we grinded together I started to ask for more.

As Taylor Dayne sang, I felt the doors to not only my body but my heart flood open with love.

"...I'll always love you for the rest of my days. You have won my heart and my soul with your sweet, sexy ways. You gave me hope when I needed someone near. You bring me happiness every day of every year. I'll always love you for all that you are. You have made my life complete, you're my lucky star..."

I began to get that feeling again, like the one earlier but this time it was stronger. I grabbed him. I began to breathe harder. The more he thrust inside me, the harder I grabbed him and the louder I called out his name.

"Money....oh, Money!"

The feeling mounted and I wrapped my legs around his waist in a death grip. I couldn't hold it. I screamed.

He held me tighter and tighter.

"Don't that feel good? You like that? You nuttin' baby, all over me. Don't it feel good?"

"Yes, yes it feels good," I responded in a shaken voice.

"Be mine, Lex. Be my girl. Let me have this…let me have you. Let me make you feel like this forever."

"I ain't going nowhere baby, you got me."

As my throbbing began to slow, his picked up. He slid his hands underneath my ass and plunged deep inside me. His thrust almost violent.

"UUUGGGGHHHHHH," he screamed.

He plopped down on top of me, juices running down my mommy, soaking the bed. He rolled over to the side of me and pulled me into his arms.

"It's never felt so good before. I hope I didn't hurt you bae."

"Pure pleasure."

We stood on the balcony, watching the sun come up. Despite the beauty of the night, I had a million questions running through my head.

Could this actually work?

I wanted it to with all my heart and as Money wrapped his arms around my wait and kissed my neck, I believed it could.

"I meant what I said, Lex. I want you. It wasn't just pillow talk."

I turned to face him.

"I know."

As the sun slid down on my face, he could see the tear falling.

"What's wrong baby?"

"I'm happy."

CHAPTER EIGHTEEN

The plan was to meet our friends at Six Flags for a day of fun. While I was waiting on Money to get out the shower I paged Muffet.

"Consider yourself lucky that you even have this number. Mother's not available at this time but if you leave yo' Southwestern Bell, I'll get back to you as soon as possible. Toodles..."

I left my message and he returned my call instantly.

"Skip the formalities honey, details... I want details. I'm assuming all went well cause it a whole new day."

"Oh Muff girl, I can't begin to tell you how sweet that man is. He is the bomb! He got me roses; he gave me a bath..."

"Gave you a bath," he interrupted. "Oh my goodness child, not all up in the creases and thangs."

"Yes honey and I did the same to him. He did everything right Muff."

"Everything?"

"E-ve-ry-thing! Oh and the rumors aren't true about nine inches either."

"Uhh, shut yo' mouth, damn!"

"It's bigger."

We laughed and I told him we'd see him in a minute.

We checked out the hotel, stopped and got a bite to eat and hit Highway 44E to join our friends at Six-Flags.

It was packed and me, Money, Muffet and his date hung out and we had a ball. We rode everything at least twice and took pictures of everything. We saw "Troop," sing live in the concert series and once again, Money made sure I had a great time.

I enjoyed myself to the fullest but there was still a small part of me that wished Tae was there.

Money and I a lot of our time together but we were also kept separate lives. I liked that. We didn't feel smothered and it gave us a chance to miss each other after school. We were working or hanging out with our friends. Money dedicated a lot of his spare time to the court and I sometimes went along to watch him play. We knew he would be getting a scholarship to college at the end of the year.

I sat and thought about Tae sometimes, wondering how she was doing and how she would feel if she knew Money and I were together. I had gone so far as to stop by and ask her mom for the number to her sister's but it was disconnected. I wanted her to hear it from me, not in the streets.

Money and Muffet was very supportive in my efforts to find her and repair our friendship. His compassion and empathy was one of the reasons I was so crazy about him. He always made me feel like I was the most important person in the world to him, so it was no surprise when the deliver guy showed up to my job with a dozen of red, long stemmed roses.

The card simply read, "Meet me in Room 112. Drury Hotel @ 7 and don't be late."

Money and I always went to the hotel to make love because we felt it would be disrespectful to do it in out parent's homes. I always got so excited when it was time for Money to make love to me.

I clocked out, rushed home and packed my overnight bag. Since I knew he'd be waiting, I wanted to give him something worth the wait. I put on a mid-thigh length, see through red night gown. I slipped on my coat and headed out the door.

When I arrived at the hotel room, the door was slightly opened. The lights were out on the inside and the sweet sounds of "Guy" playing in the background.

"...baby, you can't have all of me, cause I'm not totally. I can't tell you everything that's going on baby. There's a few things in my past that should not be explained. I'm asking you baby, be with me for a little while. Please hush, no question asked. Lay back and relax. Kick off your shoes; let your pretty sexy hair down; it's happening baby, I'm giving you a piece of me you can have..."

I entered the room and all I could see was his shadow, sitting in a chair by the window. I loved it when we role played. As I approached him he told me to stop.

"Turn around, now! Don't look back at me."

I obeyed.

He sounded a little funny but I just figured he was trying to be sexy so I played along. It was still in the room for a minute and I stood there in the middle of the room with my back turned to me. I felt his finger brush up against my neck. He placed a blindfold over my eyes. This was a new but it was kind of exciting. I could feel him walk around to the front of me.

He leaned into me and whispered in my ear.

"Well, well, well, what do you have under this coat for me?"

"Open it and see," I answered.

He pulled apart the ties that held my coat together. I let it fall off my shoulders and onto the floor His finger glided across my breast before I felt him grip them. His hands felt so big and strong against my flesh.

He slid them down my outer thighs and came back up with the bottom of my gown in his hands. He gripped my ass, firmly. He brought his body close to mine. I tried to touch him but he whispered a soft, "no" in my ear.

As he thrust his fingers inside me, he leaned in too close I guess because his earring brushed hard against my cheek.

What the fuck? Money don't have an earring!

I pushed him away, stepped back and pulled off the blindfold and almost fainted. It was Dre' standing in front of me with a smile big enough to fill an ocean.

"Dre'? What the hell is wrong with you?" I asked, bending down, picking up my coat and throwing it around me. "What the hell are you doing here?"

"I came to see you Lex, I miss you. I was wrong for letting Tae in my room that night but I promise you, I never slept with her baby. You were so mad that you jumped to conclusions and didn't give me time to defend myself."

I yanked my coat closed and tied the belt.

"Don't give me that bullshit Dre'. Save that for some other chicken head. I ain't buying it. Remember I came in your room. I saw Tae in your jersey, naked underneath. I found the open condom wrapper on the floor, remember? So don't give me that I didn't fuck her shit! And what the fuck does it even matter now?"

"Lex please listen to me baby. You got this all wrong. It's sad enough to say but the condom wrapper was old and used with someone else."

"No, I got it right Dre'. I have nothing to say to you and you have nothing to say to me. I got a man and he's twice the man you will ever be."

"You mean Money right? So it was true. I guess Tae was telling the truth about you huh?"

I walked over to the window.

178

"No, hold on, I didn't..."

"Tae told me that night that you were messing around with Money but I didn't want to believe her. Especially after all that went down and you left that night. She tried; she tried like hell to get me to fuck her but baby I promise you I didn't. I swear to you but now, hell I wish I had. It was true, all along it was true.

All these wasted nights without sleep, thinking about where you are, who you're with, what you're doing; feeling like I'm going crazy and for what? A lie?"

I walked over to him.

"Dre' I never touched Money while I was with you. This only happened after I left you. But if what you say if true, why did you let me leave assuming you had been with my best friend?"

"Again Lex, you were on a rampage with her just being there and rightfully so. I tried to talk to you, remember? I tried to call, write and everything else. You shut me down."

179

I was confused. I didn't know what to believe.

Could it be possible I was wrong? Oh my God, what if I was? I did this to Tae for no reason!

I felt lightheaded. I didn't know which way to turn. My mind said to get the hell out of there but my body wouldn't move.

He stepped closer to me and kissed me on my forehead. It felt good. He ran his hands down my cheek. It made my mommy moist. I realized that I wasn't the virgin he'd met anymore. This could quickly get out of hand.

"You miss me Lex? Am I still a part of your dreams at night? Look me in my eyes and tell me you love him."

No problem; I looked him dead in the eyes, opened my mouth but absolutely nothing would come out. I couldn't say a thing.

"That's what I thought," he said, taking me by the hand and walking me over to the bed. He sat me down, stood in front of me and began removing his clothes. His body was so cut up and I had to fight everything in me not

180

to jump his bones. My mind went to Money, undressing for me Prom night.

Dre' leaned into me and I pushed him away.

"No, Dre' I can't do this. It's too late," I said, trying not to look at the bulge in his briefs. "I do love Money."

I looked him straight in the eyes.

"More than I realized until this moment. I know he would never hurt me the way you did. He means everything to me and I won't let you come between that. Bye Dre'."

I walked to the door and he called after me. When I turned, he was standing there naked.

"You can love that nigga, fine but don't cheat yo'self, treat yo'self."

My eyes fell down to his jimmy that I could barely see. It looked as if it stopped growing at the age of ten. I thought about the Cobra my man had between his thighs and looked back at this garden snake that stood before me and chuckled.

"Oh I plan to treat myself… to a real man."

I walked out the room and closed the door behind me. I leaned up against the wall and sighed. That was a close call and I needed to go talk to Money.

I stopped by the house and changed clothes then went to see my man. I told him everything that happened and he wasn't the least bit upset. He just held me tightly in his arms.

"Temptations are everywhere baby but I love you and I trust you. Without that we have nothing."

He kissed me and every shred of doubt, every thought of Dre' was gone. I knew in my heart that this was forever.

CHAPTER NINETEEN

The next day, I couldn't wait to tell Muffet what happened.

We sat up in the lunch room on the fifth floor, having pizza and dishing the dirt.

"See, you better than me Ms. Thing cause mother would've gone "burning bed" on his ass! Better yet, knowing me, I probably would've played his game. Got down on my knees like I was about to give him some bomb head and crunch! Bit it off like a bar-be-qued Bratwurst!

That just goes to show you, men ain't shit! Just dogs tryin' to find a hole to bury they bone and *any* hole will do."

"Amen to that!" I said, high-fiving him.

"So what did Money say? Did you tell him? Did he snap out?"

"No Muff, he was good. He didn't even trip. He just said any fool would've tried to get back with me."

"Aw, damn! Why you gotta go and get the good ones?" he said, chuckling.

"You got a good one too. Wayne is a good guy and hell ya'll been tied at the hip lately."

"Yeah, boyfriends cool. He digs what I'm feeling and he don't care what his home boys say about us. He talking long term but I ain't ready for all that."

I looked at Muffet and started to slap him with a slab of pizza. I mean, how many dudes would he find willing to accept him for who he really was? He was tripping.

"Muff, you've settled for so long when we both know you deserve better. You so use to dealing with these whack ass dudes who want everything ya'll do to be on the low-low. Now here you got a nigga who ain't really giving a fuck about what somebody says? I don't see the probably.

You're about to graduate in a week and gotta think ahead, boo. I mean, seriously Muff, boosting ain't gone land you anywhere but in the pen."

His eyes perked when I mentioned jail.

"And *no*, you ain't trying to go there! Wayne's nice and he accepts you as a person, not male or female but as his companion and that should mean more to you than anything."

He puffed on his cigarette and blew the smoke out the window. I could tell I had hit a nerve. I knew that being accepted and not having to hide who he really was, was very important to Muffet.

"It does, I mean mother does like him a lot and I have been thinking about my future. I really want to go to fashion design school cause you know mother is fierce when it comes to throwing together some shit and making it hot, okay!

But Lex, he plays ball and he's good too, just like Money. What if he goes pro? He ain't about to take no fag to the Pro-Bowl, now is he?"

It hurt him to say that word. Muffet didn't see himself as a fag, society did. He saw himself as a young woman born into a man's body and forced to remain there.

"Muff, I think that if it was such a concern for him, he would've been gone a long time ago. Stop asking questions about what could happen and just enjoy the ride of what is happening now. I mean, even if it runs out of gas, it's been one hell-of-a ride, hasn't it?"

"Yes ma'am!"

We continued to talk as we walked to our next class; indulging over the men in our lives and our futures. At that moment, they looked so promising and bright for the bother of us.

The week had flown by and Money had to make his decision as to where he would be attending college the up-coming school year. He had several offers. Mizzou definitely was not an option!

We were sitting on the bleachers in Fairground Park, enjoying the breeze. He was sitting between my thighs. I knew the decision of choosing a school was weighing heavy on him.

"Lex, I've decided to stay here and go to St. Louis U. They're giving me a full ride. That way I can be here near moms," he said, turning to me. "And you. What do you think?"

I leaned down and grabbed him.

"What do I think? Money that's great! But what about Temple? I know you had your heart set on playing ball there. Your grandpa and your dad went there. I know that's your first love."

He pulled me down into his lap.

"No, you are. So, let's just get through graduation and get this life thing started, you down?"

"Hmm, last time I said that I ended up against the wall getting turned out," I laughed.

"Oh, you ain't seen nothing yet."

Graduation night had arrived and Money looked so hot in his cap and gown. I watched him across the hallway, joking around with all his friends but when he made eye contact with me, our eyes locked and I knew he felt the same attraction to me that I felt towards him.

He looked at me, undressing me with his eyes and I allowed him. Every since the first night he touched me, all it took was a glance for my body to respond in moisture.

He smiled and nodded towards the gym. I looked at the girls beside me and told them I'd be right back. I hurried across the hallway and into the gym. He was right behind me and he pulled the door closed behind him. He walked up to me and slid his hands up my thighs to my ass.

"Damn you look good. I could fuck you right here and now."

"You could?"

He looked at me with a look of surprise on his face.

"Was that a statement or a question?"

"Look at you paying attention in English class," I said, laughing and reaching under his robe, grabbing his jimmy.

He turned to look back at the door, glanced around the gym and then chose his spot. He grabbed my hand and led me up to the second level of the gym. We walked the steps and ducked off into a corner.

"You sure you want this?"

"Do I look sure?" I answered. Unzipping his slacks and reaching inside.

I grabbed his jimmy and pulled it out.

"We don't have a lot of time," I said looking him in his eyes.

He spent me around, pulled up my robe, dress and slip. He put his hand in my panties and pulled the lining to the side. His jimmy was rock solid and I was soak and wet thinking of getting caught.

He worked his way inside, talking to me along the way.

"I'm really loving the freak in you," he said, pounding inside me. "This shit feels so good."

I moaned out in ecstasy, loving the way he felt inside of me. We tried not to make any noise but as he mounted his body against mine and placed his hands on my hips, I couldn't hold it any longer.

I released a load of juices all over him and he responded with a load of his own.

We panted and tried to catch our breath.

"Come on baby, we gotta go get cleaned up. We can't be all up in graduation smelling like sex," I told him, pulling my dress down.

"I can; walk right across the stage and shake all they hands with all yo' juices on my hand."

I hit him on the shoulder and told him to come on.

As we snuck out the gym, I looked to my right and for a second I thought I saw a familiar face in the crowd but then Muffet tapped me on the shoulder before I could be sure. I turned to find Muffet giving Money some dap and I looked at Money and he winked his eye at me.

We laughed.

"Spreadin' the love baby, spreadin' the love."

CHAPTER TWENTY

The ceremony was beautiful. From the singing of, "The Greatest Love of All," to the keynote speaker, it was emotional, exciting and sorrowful. Exciting because we all were going forward with our new lives; sorrowful because we were leaving behind a place that had brought us all so much joy and happiness; emotional because I couldn't help but wish Tae were there.

When Money received his diploma, he did just as he said. He walked up, shook the principal's hand and smiled at me. He then took his tassel and turned it from the right to the left of his cap as the screams and cheers came from the crowd.

I crossed and then Muffet crossed with a Merlyn Monroe strut to die for. The crowd burst out laughing when he literally grabbed the principal and kissed him on the cheek when he handed him his diploma. She had also received his letter of acceptance to Washington University for Fashion so he was overjoyed.

After the dismissal of the graduates, our caps flew up in the air. A cloud of blue and white covered the atmosphere. I was searching for Money but as the caps began to settle, the familiar face appeared once again. It was Tae.

She looked different, very different. Our eyes met and I felt a wave of emotions flow through me. I was happy to see her, despite anything and everything that had happened.

I walked over to her but stopped about half way to her. I looked at her and the difference became crystal clear. She was pregnant. I could only begin to imagine by whom; probably some guy who was now doing time and left her out here hanging by herself.

We stopped within arms' reach.

"Hey," she said with a half smile.

"Hey Tae, I see you've been busy," I said, nodding towards her stomach.

"Umm, is there somewhere we can go to talk Lex? I really need to talk to you and I know this ain't the best time but it's really important."

I looked at her, unsure of how to respond.

"Please Lex; can I just come by later on?"

She noticed Money off in the crowd. She watched him as she twirled the charm around on her necklace.

"I see Money still looking good. He's…"

"We're together Tae," I blurted out, interrupting her before she got too caught up in thinking things could probably work out between them.

It wasn't the way I wanted her to find out but it just sort of flew out when I saw the desire in her eyes for Money.

"We've been together since prom. We got a good thing going."

I stepped closer to her. If she was going to fly off the handle and make a scene, I wanted to be ready. My grandmother and other family members were there and I wasn't going to allow her to clown.

"Look Tae, I'm really sorry that all this happened between us all. Money makes me happy but I didn't go after him it just..."

"It's okay Lex, really. I kind of figured that day after the title game that it would happen eventually. It wasn't the way he *didn't* look at me but the way he *did* look at you. Hey," she said reaching for my arm. "It should've been you two all along. I really do wish you both the best. I'm just glad to see you. Truth is I've missed you so much."

I pulled her to me and we embraced. It felt so good to hug my girl after all the drama.

"Oh, I've missed you too Tae. Prom night was like..."

Just then, Money grabbed me around my waist from behind and kissed me on my neck.

"Ummmmm... congratulations baby!" he said, placing a juicy kiss on my lips.

"Congratulations baby! Look who's here."

Money swallowed the lump in his throat and looked at Tae; noticing the small pumpkin sized belly in the front. He looked back to me, unsure of what to do or what to say. I broke the ice between them.

"I told her about us baby and she's happy for us. Isn't that great? Don't she look great?" I said nudging him.

He cleared his throat.

"Hey Tae, how you been?"

"I'm good Money. Congrats, on both your graduation and your relationship. I'm really happy for you two."

There was an awkward moment of silence in the air.

"Well, good to see you Tae."

He kissed me again.

"I'm going to find moms. We all heading out to Red Lobster, you going right?"

"I really need to talk to Tae for a minute, do you mind heading without me. I'll meet you guys there shortly."

"Okay but don't be too long baby, it's time to celebrate."

He leaned into my ear and whispered, "I'm glad you got her back."

I smiled.

He kissed me on the cheek and then surprised Tae and me when he walked over to her and placed a kiss on her cheek as well.

"It really is good to see you Tae. We've all been worried about you and missing you. Take care and don't be a stranger."

We watched him walk away.

"Always the gentlemen," she said.

"So, Tae what's up? What's so important?"

Before she could start talking Muffet walked up and being the drama queen that he is, lit into Tae something terrible.

"Oh no you didn't Ms. Thing! You did not have the gall to show up here with yo' trifflin' ass to our graduation after what you did to my Lex! You…"

"Muff…:

"It's okay honey, I got this one," he said, twirling her neck and pointing his finger in Tae's face. "You are so tired! Oh look," he said, pointing to Tae's stomach. "The fish has caviar. You ain't shit but a lil' piece of tripe sitting in the snack shop waiting for anybody to pick yo' ass up! If I was her, I would've knocked yo' ass out."

Tae flinched back and I grabbed Muffet by the arm.

"Muff chill! It's graduation. I got this. Gone over there with Wayne, he's waiting for you. I can handle this. Go now, please."

He hesitantly began to walk away.

"You lucky I'm feeling real lady like this evening."

I grabbed Tae by the arm and began to lead her out of the auditorium. I stopped to speak with my Nana briefly, take some pictures and then proceeded to talk with Tae.

"Don't trip off Muff, you know how he gets. So, you were saying?"

"Well you can see one of my problems but that ain't the worst of it. I've been thinking about you so much Lex. The way things went down. I miss the relationship we had.

I was wrong Lex. I apologize for crossing you. You were like... no, you were my sister and I hurt you. For that I am truly sorry. Lex, DeAndre'..."

I put up my hand.

"I don't wanna talk about that Tae."

"But Lex..." she pleaded.

"That's it, I'm out of here. You come here thinking what Tae? That I'd be ready to hear all about your wild and crazy night with Dre'. Well you're wrong. I don't wanna here nothing about his dog ass.

I mean what, next you'll tell me he's yo' baby's daddy. I don't have time for this," I said waving my hand and turning to walk away.

"He gave me HIV Lex!"

I spun around so fast I was light headed. Did she just say what I think she said?

"What? Who gave you what? What do you mean, HIV? How did…"

I was standing with my mouth wide open. I was in complete shock.

"Dre, the bastard infected me."

What?

I almost fainted when it came out of her mouth.

Infected? Dre'? HIV? What the fuck?

I was stunned but for more reasons than she could ever imagine. He had lied to me that night at the hotel. He had slept with Tae and he was trying to sleep with me too.

The muthafucka was trying to infect me too? That son-of-a-bitch! But why; why would he purposely try to infect me?

"I have HIV Lex. The condom we used broke and I got both infected and pregnant. I've known for a couple of months now which is why I haven't been back to school."

Her voice began to break.

"I couldn't bring myself to tell you. I didn't know what you would say. I was afraid you'd tell me that I deserve every bit of it, so I stayed away. But I feel so alone and I couldn't stay away any longer. I'm scared and I need a friend, my friend."

I was enraged but I ached for Tae. It was unfair that one mistake could have such dire consequences. In one instance, one act, she lost her virginity, got pregnant and contracted HIV. I wanted to kill him for what he did to the both of us. The old cliché came to mind that my Nana used

201

to say to my grand-dad when she caught him looking at other women.

"Everything that looks good *to* you ain't good *for* you!"

I walked over to her and wrapped my arms around her. She began to cry even harder. I hurt for her and the baby.

"Wait, if you're positive, what about the baby?"

She rubbed her stomach.

"I've been taking medication to try to prevent her from catching it from me. I had to tell you. I need you Lex, I need you."

I squeezed her tightly and a tear rolled down my face. I was hurting for tae but I was also crying at the realization that this could have very well been me. I was thanking God silently.

"All that stuff is in the past girl. I'm here for you now and I'm not going anywhere. I love you Tae and we'll get through this, together."

"My life is over Lex, what am I gone do?"

You're gone let us help take care of you and my little niece or nephew. Money and I can..."

"Oh no Lex, please don't tell Money. Please don't tell anybody. I don't want anybody treating me like I got the plague. Promise me you won't say anything."

Okay," I sighed. "For now I'll keep it to myself. So where are you staying? You still across the river with your sister?"

She shook her head.

"Yeah and I probably won't come back this way again so I'll call you and give you the address and phone number so maybe you can come visit me on the Ill side. I just wanted to come and tell you what was going on with me and well, to tell you I love you."

"I love you to Tae. Hey, before you go, why don't you come eat with us or at least let me take you home."

"That's okay, I got my sister bug over there, I'll be fine."

We chuckled. It was good to see her laugh. I had missed her so much.

"Besides, Money's waiting for you. Go be with your man girl, I'm fine. I really am happy for you. I'll see you soon, ok?"

"Okay, you will, I promise."

I watched her walk away towards her car and my heartfelt extremely heavy. I had to do everything I could to help her.

"Tae," I yelled. "Call me, I'll be waiting."

She waved and then disappeared across the way. I wiped the tears from my face and thought how lucky I was to have made the choice I made. In a sad twist of fate, Tae's betrayal had saved my life. Yet, I hate she had to go through was she was going through.

I jumped in my car and headed to meet Money and our friends at Red Lobster. As I drove off the parking lot of Cooks' Sporting Goods Store, I wondered what the future held for all of us, especially Tae.

EPILOGUE

Six years have come and gone so fast. Seems like just yesterday, we were all care free spirits wondering the halls of the "V," Now here we are, grown-ups with grown up responsibilities.

Money and I are married. Two years now and I thank God for him every day. He's the best thing that has ever happened to me. We're expecting our first child any day now. He finished college and used his athletic scholarship to study medicine and he's continuing his education to be a doctor.

I'm finishing up my nursing degree at Harris Stowe State University where I'm currently on the Honor Roll. I lost my Nana a few years back but thanks to Money, I now have my father back in my life and we go to visit him once a month. He is scheduled for released in a few months and I can't wait for him to be a part of our lives.

Muffet graduated from Washington University with a degree in fashion and now working at Famous Barr. He is bad too. He is looking to start his own clothing line soon.

A lot of blessings have come my way in my lifetime but the most important one was seeing that day at graduation. I thought I'd lost her forever but she did call and I spent the next six months of her pregnancy, much to Muffet's disgrace, helping her keep appointments.

She stayed sick a lot but thankfully the baby was born perfectly healthy. Sadly, a few months after Kamay Latriece Jackson turned three, I stared to painfully watch Tae deteriorate right before my eyes.

I hated Dre' for what he'd done. He was later brought up on charges for knowingly infecting women with the virus. Every time I thought of him, I looked to Money and smiled. If it wasn't for his love for me, I may have strayed and I could've been one of his victims.

It was so unfair that he was still here and Tae was gone but one blessing came out from all the lies and betrayal and that's Kamay. She Tae's alright; clings to Money like glue. I guess you really can't change genetics huh? She reminds me of Tae so much; her eyes, her smile and definitely her attitude.

She's forever a part of me because Tae was a part of me; sister's til' the end... Still and always, my best friend!

SNEAK PREVIEW

MIMIKA AVENUE II... The Game Has Changed

Mystic sat in the back row of Ronald Jones' Funeral Chapel and reached down inside her purse for a tissue. The tears fell from her eyes for many reasons. It had been a week since Spider had walked out on her after finding out about her sleeping with Remy, one of his business partners.

He was so livid with her that he couldn't even begin to wrap his mind around the fact that she had also told him that she was carrying his child.

He hadn't spoken to her since that evening. Normally he would ride up and down the block several times a day but since that day; he'd been going to the store using the back route.

The block hadn't been the same since all the madness had gone down. It wasn't totally quiet but eerily silent. Something was definitely different and Mystic's world had changed forever.

She dabbed the liquid flowing from her eyes as she focused in on Spider sitting close to the front pew with his wife beside him.

Her heart was torn apart at the site of him, leaning on her shoulder. It should be her, she reasoned. After all, it was her who legs he lay between when Get Down lost his life. It was her who did whatever she had to do to post his bond and it had been her who kept his secret of what happened the night Man's cousin was murdered.

She had his back but his ego and status in the hood was bruised and to Spider, that meant more than anything to him, including her.

Mystic shifted her eyes to the podium where one of the church members stood with the microphone in her hand. Her voice was so powerful despite coming from a 5'2 inch frame. She sounded angelic as she sent a wave of emotion through the chapel.

"... How do I say to goodbye, to what we had? The good times that made us laugh outweighed the bad. I thought we'd live

to see forever but forever has gone away. It's so hard to say goodbye, to yesterday…"

Mystic cried at the thought of not seeing Lil' Curtis again. He always made her laugh. She chuckled through the tears as she thought of him walking up the block in his pink bath robe, boxers and knee high tube socks. She would miss him.

Her eyes drifted back to Spider who was clearly shaken by the words of the song. Mystic knew he wasn't just crying for Lil' Curtis but for his friends, Kay and Get Down. He was still locked up and didn't get to attend Get Down's funeral.

She wanted so badly to run over to him, push his wife out the way, grab him and hold him close tom her. In her heart she still believed that it was her he wanted and needed, not his wife.

As the stood to walk around and view the body, Mystic got a chance to see him up close and personal. Her heart raced as he came closer and closer to her. They made eye contact and while Mystic's heart leaped, Spider reached back and grabbed his wife's hand to pull her closer to him. He knew this would hurt Mystic. He passed her and looked at her and quickly turned away, hugging his wife.

Mystic's heart sank to her stomach. She felt nauseated. She had to get out of there and throw up. She gathered her belonging's, cut through the oncoming line of people and walked out the chapel.

She ran down the steps the basement restroom, into the stall and spilled her guts. She hurled into the toilet through tears and hurt. She stood up, walked over to the sink, gathered a handful of cool water and splashed it on her face. She dabbed herself with a paper towel.

When she exited the bathroom she was walking with her eyes to the floor. She felt his hand touch her shoulder. She looked up at him and felt herself being pulled into his arms. She felt so emotional when he wrapped his arms around her and she laid her head on his shoulder and cried.

He rubbed her back and told her that it would be okay.

"Let that shit out."

He pulled her face to his and wiped her eye.

"You aight?" he whispered.

"Yeah… thanks, Man."

OTHER NOVELS BY ALLYSHA HAMBER:

Keep It On the Down Low, Nobody Has to Know

What's Done in the Dark

The Northside Clit

Mimika Avenue

Unlovable Bitch, A Hoe is born

Unlovable Bitch 2, Redemption or Revenge

*AVAILABLE NOW @

www.amazon.com, Barnes&Noble.com, Books-A-Million, Walden Books or check your local book store.

COMING SOON:

Mimika Avenue Part 2

Federal Prison Camp, Only the Strong Can Survive

Unlovable Bitch Part 3, I know I've Been Changed

The Clean Up Man

215

All I want for Christmas, Is Her Man